Published by Commonwealth Education Trust Books
80 Haymarket, London SW1Y 4TE, United Kingdom
www.cet1886.org

Second edition published, 2012
This collection first published, 2011

Produced for the Commonwealth Education Trust by The StoryWorks Ltd
www.thestoryworks.me.uk
Printed and bound in China by 1010 Printing International Limited
Production by Bonnie Murray at Third Millennium Information Ltd

ISBN Paperback: 978-0-9569299-3-8

Jan Pieńkowski

A River of Stories

Tales and Poems from Across the Commonwealth

Compiled by Alice Curry

Foreword by His Royal Highness The Prince of Wales

COMMONWEALTH
EDUCATION TRUST

Dedicated to the children of
The Commonwealth of Nations
in celebration of the
125th Anniversary of the
foundation of the
Commonwealth Education Trust

All profits will go towards supporting the educational purposes of the Trust

Contents

Contents

© Mario Testino

A Message From His Royal Highness The Prince of Wales

Books are very special. For some of us, of course, literature can now be pulled up on a screen as easily as music can be downloaded, and the advantages of such accessible web-based resources are undoubted. But just as a map has a beauty and even a mystery that can never be caught by a satellite-navigation system, so a book has a personality, a presence and a permanence which electronic devices would struggle to convey.

The special quality of the written word – its power and its magic – comes together in this anthology of poems, tales and myths from around the Commonwealth which are united by the theme of water. And like all good fiction, these stories serve the purpose of enhancing and explaining reality. They help us reflect on the huge challenges we face – from climate change to the depletion of natural resources and eco-systems, and from food security to unsustainable population growth. As a result, these stories encourage us to think about the kind of future we will pass on to our children and grandchildren, and the central importance of water to that future.

Fiction also enables us to think imaginatively about our reality and the challenges it presents. Nature functions as a single and integrated whole, and this is how we need to approach water. It is only by taking a holistic approach to water management that we will be able to meet our needs while, at the same time, maintaining the natural systems that are essential for our continued welfare.

There are many examples of communities that have approached water management in a holistic way. For centuries, some communities have harvested rainfall and irrigated crops through highly efficient systems. The success of these methods has, in some cases, been enhanced through the conservation of trees, which help recharge streams and groundwater. Other communities have demonstrated how composted crop wastes can improve soils so they hold water for longer. Of course, modern technology has a vital part to play but, in the end, it is how we see our relationship with Nature that will have the biggest impact on our long-term future, and that is why I think this book is so important.

The publication of this anthology marks the 125th anniversary of the original trust fund which was raised by my great, great grandfather, as Prince of Wales, who later became King Edward VII, from subscriptions from the people of the Commonwealth of Nations to further education and research. I do hope you will enjoy the beautiful writing and illustrations found in these pages, and that you are inspired to find the wisdom that is needed to take the world forward in a sustainable way for the next 125 years.

ABOUT THE WORDS

Stories and poems are like rivers: they flow from country to country. Tales flowing from ear to ear might change style or length or form, but they will always retain the flavour of their origins: the tastes, sights and smells of the lands from which they sprang. Stories and poems can encourage children to learn about the world of other children, in other places, at other times and in other circumstances, for tales, like rivers, are ever-flowing and ever-changing. A *River of Stories* uses water as its theme to celebrate such imaginative cultural connection.

Water, an essential component in everyone's lives, has a different meaning for each one of us. For children in desert-swathed Africa and monsoon-lashed Asia, the words 'drought' and 'flood' have very different implications. A culture's relationship with water might be a joy or a struggle; it might remain unvaried for centuries or else be in constant need of adaptation to a changing climate. Human stories, along with those of the animals who share our planet and the spirits and deities nourished for centuries by our beliefs, are set against a backdrop of the waters that sustain us.

Like a boat setting sail, this collection of myths, folktales, contemporary stories and poems charts a course from the land to the open seas, negotiating tempestuous elements and stormy skies, before finally weighing anchor amongst the mystical and fantastic beings of legend who attempt (and sometimes fail!) to control the capricious elements. In moving from the mundane to the mythical, the collection illuminates the ways in which water can inspire our imaginations, generation after generation.

I hope the adventures of bickering crabs, greedy pirates, boastful water gods and lonely rain goddesses will inspire the children amongst you to think a little more deeply about our water-washed world. Perhaps these tales will continue their flow beyond this collection into libraries, classrooms and playgrounds near and far, changing style and form as they adapt to new cultures. Above all, I hope you will enjoy reading these tales as much as I have enjoyed collecting them.

Alice Curry

ABOUT THE PICTURES

Jan Pieńkowski is one of Britain's best-loved illustrators, with over a hundred titles to his name. His career has spanned several decades during which he has captured the nation's heart with favourite characters, his pioneering of the modern pop-up book, and with his dramatic and beautiful silhouettes.

Jan was born in Warsaw in 1936 into a family of architects and artists. The war made his childhood an adventure, if not a comfortable one at times, taking him from Poland to Austria, Germany, Italy and finally to England in 1946, where his father sent him to a boarding school, knowing this would make him learn English if he wanted to survive. He did survive and went on to read Classics and English at King's College Cambridge, where his love of story and art, travel and history were cemented.

It was at King's that he began his design career, creating posters for university theatre productions. They were often pinched off the notice boards before the shows opened but led to a career in design for advertising, TV and publishing. He wrote and illustrated children's books in his spare time but the books soon took over and he became twice winner of the *Library Association Kate Greenaway Medal*.

Jan felt it was an honour to be asked to create pictures for this book and also a great challenge. He has often used the drawings from his sketchbooks that captured his rich experiences during travels in all parts of the world: in the story from Malaysia, for instance, the swinging monkey is from sketches of a tribe of monkeys migrating from one huge tree to another, squabbling over their babies. His trademark silhouette style has brought a visual unity to these poems and stories from more than fifty countries.

Jan works at home in his attic studio overlooking the river Thames. He hears the rain – and sometimes the hail – on his skylights, and from the windows he can see the blue sails of the racing dinghies scudding up and down the river.

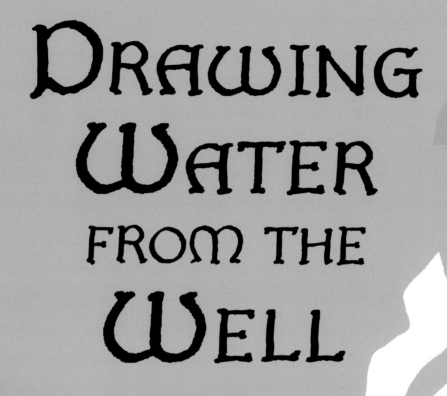

DRAWING WATER FROM THE WELL

BOTSWANA

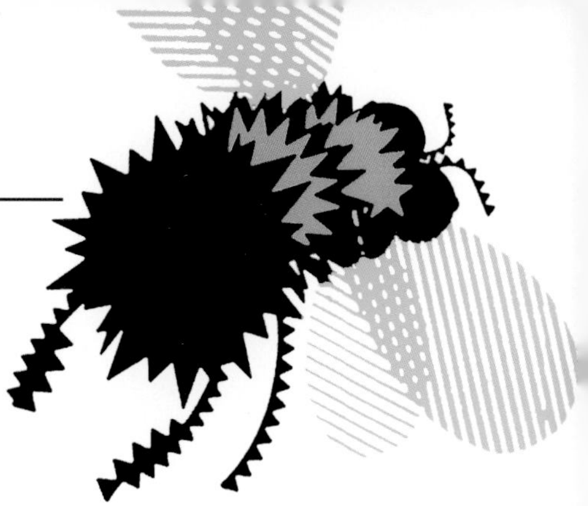

Woman's World

By Barolong Seboni

Silhouetted
against the setting sun
women
ascend
a hilly incline
balancing
barrels on their heads

talking laughing
with hardly a
splash...

the world
rotates
on the axis
of the earth's women

talking laughing
at life
with oceans
balanced
on their heads
without
a
splash...

Cooking with Salt Water

Retold by Pleasant DeSpain

ong, long ago, when the islands were ruled by the great chiefs Sun and Sea, an old woman named Amara excelled at growing and cooking vegetables. Amara's village was located near the top of a steep volcanic mountain overlooking the ocean. Each day the old woman cooked savoury dishes while gazing out upon the blue and green water far, far below.

Old Amara feared the sea. Long before, when she was a child, her warrior father paddled his canoe into a raging storm and never returned. Amara's mother said that Chief Sea swallowed him up because he was angry with her father. Amara kept away from the sea's anger by staying on the mountain her entire life. She let the braver villagers climb down the steep path to the ocean shore to catch fat fish and find valuable shells. The old woman traded her vegetables and cooking skills for a share of the bounty, and thus she survived.

One day Amara ran out of salt. She made a sour face and said, "I must have salt for my cooking pot. Without it, my food tastes as plain as a banana peel. I'll borrow some from my neighbour."

Amara's neighbour couldn't help her out, however, as she, too, was out of salt. Even worse, there was no salt to be found in the entire village. The salt trader wasn't scheduled to return to the village for an entire month. The people complained of their bad fortune.

Old Amara began to think. "A month without salt is a serious matter," she decided. "Chief Sea has an abundance of salt, more than he needs. If I cooked my food in sea water, I wouldn't have to buy salt from the trader. I'd enjoy delicious meals, and be the envy of everyone in the village. I'll have to be brave to face the ocean for the first time. I'll leave early in the morning, before anyone else is up. Cooking with salt water is a wonderful idea! Why didn't I think of it before?"

At dawn's first light, Amara wrapped her largest water gourd in a finely woven coconut fibre net, slung it over her back, and started down the steep mountain trail. It was a long journey for such thin, old legs, and she stopped to rest several times. At last she arrived at the edge of the ocean.

Amara was frightened. Up close, Chief Sea was much larger than she had realised. She tried not to stand too near, but it was high tide, and the cool water lapped at her dusty feet. This, and the soothing sound of the ocean, like a giant seashell pressed to her ear, helped to calm her.

With a shaky voice, Amara said, "I'll fill my gourd, if you don't mind, Chief Sea. I won't take very much. Thank you for your generosity."

She held the empty gourd under water and watched the air bubbles escape. When it was full, she stopped up the hole with banana leaves, and slung the gourd onto her back. It was heavy work for an old woman, but with the aid of a stout walking stick, Amara began the long climb home.

"I hope Chief Sea doesn't miss the salt water I've taken," she said to herself as she climbed. "He has so much and I've taken so little."

Due to the heavy load, the path seemed twice as steep on the way up. Old Amara had to rest after every one hundred steps. At midday she reached a lookout point, halfway up the mountain.

"I've a long way to go, but I'll make it before nightfall. The path is well marked from here to the village. Again, I'll give thanks to Master Sea, and then go home with my prize."

Amara looked out and down at the ocean, and let out a scream! Chief Sea had shrunk! Bare sand was visible for as far as she could see. Trembling with fear, the old woman asked, "What have I done? I took just a little salt water, but much more is gone. Chief Sea will be furious. What will I do? What will I do?"

Having never before left the mountain, the poor woman knew nothing

of tides, and how they rise and fall. From the great height of her village, she couldn't tell the difference between a high tide and a low tide. From this vantage point, however, she saw a much smaller sea, and was frightened for her life.

Amara thought for a long moment and said, "I must give it back. Please, Mighty Sea, hold on to your anger. Give me time to climb back down to you, and I'll return what I've taken."

Fuelled by fear, Amara quickly struggled down the mountain trail, the heavy gourd bouncing against her bony back. Just as Chief Sun began to set, Amara's feet finally touched the sand. She walked out to the water's edge and emptied the gourd into the sea.

"I didn't mean to take so much, Chief Sea. Please forgive me for my foolishness. I'll go home, now, and never again will I steal from you."

Amara hurried back up the path just as fast as her exhausted legs could carry her. She stopped to rest at the lookout, halfway up the mountain. Again, Amara gazed down at the ocean. The night sky provided just enough light for her to see the water lapping gently up to the beach's highest point. Although she didn't realise it, the tide was in.

The old woman was greatly relieved. "Chief Sea cannot be angry with me now that I've filled him up again. I'll have to cook without salt for the month ahead, just like the other villagers. Such is life."

She continued her journey home in the dark. Never again did Amara venture down to the sea.

Prescription

By Emma Kruse Va'ai

Gather some sunshine
and warm rain
one cicada
and a pocket of air from your kitchen
a pot pourri of frangipani, sandalwood, mosooi
and gardenia
into a parcel
with a long letter
airmail
to me
from you
home in Samoa

Do You Believe in Magic?

By Saviour Pirotta

hen Sumed came back from holiday, he brought a seashell with him. "It's a magic shell," he said. "I found it on the beach at midnight."

Linda held the shell to her ear.

"I can hear the sea," she cried.

"No," said Miss Wicks, "it's not the sea you can hear."

"It is," said Leroy, taking the shell from Linda. "I can hear it too. It's breaking on the shore and making a crashing sound."

Miss Wicks sighed patiently: "I know it *sounds* like the sea. But it's not."

Before she could explain, Sunita took the shell from Leroy and held it to her ear.

"Goodness me," she said. "I'm sure I can hear dolphins jumping in and out of the sea."

"Don't be silly," laughed Miss Wicks. "You can't hear dolphins jump."

"You can hear these ones," Sunita insisted. "They go CHLI-FF when they jump and CHLU-FF when they fall back in the water."

"You're joking," cried Peter who was mad about dolphins. "Let me try. Yes, I can hear dolphins. And I can hear fishermen too. Their oars are splashing in the waves."

"Your ears are playing tricks on you," said Miss Wicks, who was pretty sure Class 5 were playing tricks on her.

"But I can hear them too!" yelled Wilma. "There are waves and boats and fish. I can hear birds too: just listen!"

Miss Wicks smiled and said, "No one can hear so many sounds in a shell."

Wilma looked a bit cross and handed the shell to Dith Tu. Dith was a quiet and clever boy. His imagination couldn't run away with him.

"I can hear the sea," Dith said quietly. "And the fish, the boats and the birds. I can hear the wind in the trees too. There are big trees on the beach. They must be like the ones back home."

"It's true," said Charlene, putting the shell to her ear. "There's the sea and the fish, the birds, the wind in the trees. I can hear dogs barking too. They must be chasing the waves."

"Nonsense!" Miss Wicks shook her head.

"Charlene is right," shouted Raymond. "There are dogs barking on the beach. There are children too. They're playing sand games on the beach and they're swimming."

"There must be a little bit of my granny's village caught in the shell," said Sumed, holding the shell to his ear. "I can hear grown-ups too. They're working and singing and calling to the children to be careful."

"Look, Class 5, it's a lovely shell," said Miss Wicks, "but there's nothing in it – there can't be."

"But there is," chanted Class 5. "You have a go at listening, Miss."

"I don't need to have a go," said Miss Wicks firmly. "I *know* there can be nothing in it." She dropped the shell in the fish tank and took Class 5 out to play.

"Poor Miss," Sumed whispered to Wilma. "She *should* believe in magic."

The Boy Who Called Across the River

Adapted from a retelling by W. R. E. Clarke

nce upon a time there was a boy called Ndapi. One day his mother told him to go to the river and call his brother, who was on the other side. When Ndapi stood on the bank of the river and began calling his brother, he heard a voice on the other side calling in exactly the same way he had.

Now Ndapi was a proud boy and assumed that the other boy was making fun of him. He called out, "Who is mocking me over there?"

The Voice replied, "Who is mocking me over there?"

Ndapi cried out, "You come over here and show yourself!"

And again the Voice came, "You come over here and show yourself!"

This made Ndapi angrier than ever and he shouted out, "Boy! Come out!"

And the Voice called, "Boy! Come out!"

When Ndapi found that he could not cross the river, he returned home to his mother and told her all about it, saying, "Mother, as I was calling my brother a very proud and arrogant boy on the other side of the river began to mock me. I challenged him to come and meet me face to face, but he would not come."

When she heard this his mother laughed and said to him, "Ndapi, you were challenging yourself, because it was your own voice coming back to you in an echo!"

Wednesday Afternoon

By Karlo Mila

my father is "having fun"
cleaning the floor
he uses the plugged-in sink as a bucket
wears rags on his feet
and shimmies to a cleaning beat
he asks me to read the label
on the bottle for him
he wants our floor to shine
and laughs when (surprise)
it does
this is how I will remember him
moonwalking across our kitchen floor
rags under his feet
"that's how my mother taught me"
he says
"but I never take any note
it takes me forty years to do what she say"

The Magic Fish

Retold by Ann Walton *(Abridged)*

here was once a little boy called Yusuf who helped his father prepare the nets for fishing every morning. Yusuf had a fishing rod of his own, and after his father sailed away over the lake in the morning, Yusuf would bait the hook with a worm and wait for a fish to bite. If he caught one, Yusuf took a chambo home for his mother to cook.

One day, as his father set off across the still dark lake before sunrise, Yusuf settled down on the shore. He baited his hook with a worm and waited for a bite. Almost at once, even before he had a chance to daydream a little, he hooked a great big fish that almost jumped out of the water and into his hands. It was the biggest fish that Yusuf had ever caught. In fact it was bigger than any fish that his father had ever caught! Yusuf dropped it into his bag and ran home to give it to his mother to cook for supper. On the way, he met Goodwill, his friend.

"Look here, Goodwill, I have caught a fish. It is the biggest fish that I have ever seen!" Yusuf put the bag down, and opened it. Goodwill looked inside. He shook his head.

"You are crazy, Yusuf. Why do you say you have a great big fish when you have a great big guinea fowl? You are a great big liar, Yusuf!" And with those words, Goodwill went on his way. Yusuf quickly looked into the bag to see for himself. Goodwill was right. He had a guinea fowl, the biggest one that he had ever seen. And it winked at him. Yusuf closed the bag quickly and ran home to give the guinea fowl to his mother. On the way he met Watchman, another of his friends.

"Look here, Watchman. I have caught a guinea fowl. It is the biggest guinea fowl that I have ever seen!" Yusuf put the bag down, and opened it. "See for yourself, Watchman! Have you ever seen such a great big guinea fowl?" Watchman looked inside. Then he looked at Yusuf, and he shook his head.

"You are crazy, Yusuf! Why do you say you have a great big guinea fowl when you have a great big goat? You are a great big liar, Yusuf!" And with those words Watchman went on his way. Yusuf again looked into the bag to see for himself. Watchman was right. He had a goat, the biggest one he had ever seen. And it winked at him. Yusuf closed the bag and ran home to his mother.

"Look here, Mama! I have caught a goat. It is the biggest goat that I have ever seen! Yusuf put the bag down, and opened it. "See for yourself Mama! Have you ever seen such a great big goat?" Mama looked inside and laughed.

"Why do you say you have a great big goat when you have a great big fish? Silly boy! But thank you for the great big fish for our supper, Yusuf!"
Then Mama put her arms around Yusuf and gave him a great big kiss. Yusuf couldn't believe his ears. He looked into the bag to see for himself. Mama was right. He had a fish. It was the same great big fish that he had caught at sunrise. It really was the biggest fish he had ever seen. And it didn't wink at him.

While Mama cooked the great big fish for supper that night, Yusuf told his father about the great big fish that had turned into a great big guinea fowl, and about the great big guinea fowl that had turned into a great big goat, and about the great big goat that had turned back into the great big fish. When he had finished his father looked at him.

"You are a very good fisherman, Yusuf. And you are also a great big storyteller!" Yusuf smiled. At least his father hadn't called him a great big liar!

Why People Have to Die

Retold by Bo Flood et al.

nce there was a young boy who loved his grandmother very much. He was so small she often held his hand as they walked. Every day they walked under the leafy forest canopy to the bathing pool. There, the river was wide and slow. On the day that changed human lives forever, the birds were singing, "treee-kik, treee-kik." It was spring, and purple trumpet-flowers lifted their open faces to the sun. No one knew that death was coming.

The grandmother spread her best woven mat on the ground. She sat the child on it. "Stay here while I bathe," she said. "The river is cool, clear, and deep. Don't go in the water. Just wait for me."

Then she did a shocking thing. She crawled out from inside her old skin. It was full of wrinkles and hung limply around her knees and elbows. Even her cheeks sagged, like overripe fruit. The grandmother dropped her old skin on the ground as if she were throwing away the empty husk of a coconut. "I'll be back soon," she said to her little grandson. Then she slipped into the cool, fresh water.

Sunlight sparkled on the water. Her grandson watched her splash. Soon she was clean, and she came back to him. "You see," she said, "I wasn't gone long, was I?"

He didn't answer. He stared at her with terrified eyes.

"Let's go. I'll take you home to your brothers now." The boy stared and stared. His lip began to tremble. He had never seen his grandmother without her skin. He didn't recognise this young woman. Her skin was young and tight, like his own. Her face was rosy and smooth. She was pretty, but he didn't want to go with her. Not this stranger. When she reached out her hand for his, he shrank down against the ground.

"What?" she said. "Are you afraid of me, my little one? I'm your grandmother. Do you think you don't know me? Remember when we picked berries in the woods? How you found fire ants inside that rotting log? How we sang the starling's song?"

The little boy was too scared to speak. He wanted only one thing: for his own grandmother to come back. He didn't like this strange woman at all.

His grandmother sat down next to him. Her head hung down in sorrow. How much she wanted to be young and beautiful again! But she knew now that it couldn't be. She sighed a long, deep sigh. Gently, she picked up her old, wrinkled skin and dusted it off. Slowly, she put it on again. Her face sagged. Her brow was lined with age and worry. Her young feet became flat and stiff to walk on. Even her belly swelled out in front of her.

The old woman sighed. "For the love of the children, so it must be."

Down
by the
Water
Hole

The Enchanted River Tree

Retold by Tom Nevin *(Abridged)*

It is in a green and peaceful land, along the banks of a great river that our story takes place. It was a time long, long ago when humans and animals lived side by side as friends and neighbours. Most of the time they got on pretty well.

The humans had built their village not far from the great river. Of course, they were careful not to build their homes too close to the water, for summer storms brought huge thunder clouds, lightning, wild winds and pouring rain.

One solitary tree defied the wind, the rain and the destructive flood waters. Looking quite dead, no leaves sprouted from the dry black branches as they reached up into the sky, nor were buds or shoots ever seen on its hard, wooden skin. Standing alone on the bank of the river, the great tree ignored completely the highest and most powerful floods that tried to tear it down.

It was said the tree was bewitched. How the tree came to be that way, no one could say for sure, but the people and the animals agreed that anything able to withstand the fury of an African storm must surely have supernatural powers.

Only one animal lived in that dark and lifeless place. He was Kala, the otter. Unlike the other animals, Kala had no fear of this tree. It was safe and dry and he lived a life of uninterrupted peace.

Kala was a water-loving animal. He had a sleek, narrow body that made him a natural swimmer and enabled him to cut through the water at an amazing speed. Kala also had a very healthy appetite. Not only did he enjoy his dinners of tiger fish, vundu and bream, but he also had a particular liking for fresh corn. Nor could he resist the delicious flavour of groundnuts, or the plump dark-green melons full of sweet juice.

The problem was that the corn, the nuts and the melons belonged to an old woman of the village. She and her beautiful daughter worked hard in the fields every day, lovingly tending their crops to make them grow full and healthy. So, you should not be surprised to learn that they became very angry at Kala's repeated raids. What were they to do?

Late one afternoon the old woman was sitting outside her house gazing down at the river. The tall black tree that was Kala's home was stark and forbidding. Suddenly she sat up.

"That's it! That's the answer!" she exclaimed out loud. "To be rid of the otter, we must get rid of the tree. Somewhere in this land there is someone strong enough and brave enough to bring down that tree. I shall offer you as the bride to the one who can get the job done."

Word travelled fast, as it does in Africa. Before long, the boldest and most powerful men and animals came to demolish the tree. Do not be shocked to hear that the animals of the forest and the plains were also there, for in those long ago days it was not at all unusual for humans to marry animals.

The first to test his strength was a handsome young warrior. He had spent the night polishing and honing the blade of his big axe until it was as sharp as a razor. Now the warrior stood before the tree, lifted his axe and swung it with all his strength. It left not the smallest mark. Again he swung the great axe, again and again. Finally he had to give up and went sadly home.

Next in line was Elephant. What a big fellow he was! Surely the old tree would be no match for his massive shoulders and huge tusks. Elephant raised his head and gave a deafening trumpeting cry. Wrapping his trunk around the tree, he leaned against it and began to push. Everyone held their breath. Elephant shoved and heaved but the old tree did not budge. He tried again, and once again after that, but still the tree stood firm. Exhausted he stamped angrily back into the bush.

Lion was next. Now we shall see, thought the old woman. Lion is king of the beasts and no-one, not even a bewitched tree, can withstand him. The great lion, a thick golden mane flowing from his massive shoulders, walked slowly and with much majesty up to the tree. He took a deep breath and let out the most terrifying roar. There, he thought, that should do it. When the tree did not immediately fall over he was most surprised. Lion took an even deeper breath and let out an even louder roar. But it was no good. There was not the slightest movement. Lion knew that he too had failed and with as much dignity as he could muster, he too walked away.

Rhinoceros watched, awaiting his turn. Now the great animal lowered his horned head and began to run. Faster and faster he went and when he hit the tree full square he was travelling at top speed. The bush echoed with the sound of the collision, the very ground shook. Rhino shook his head, took a few paces back and looked at the tree in disbelief. It was still standing. Disgruntled, he walked back, took an even longer run and slammed once more into the tree. CRRRRAAAASHHHH! Still the tree stood. Rhino retreated into the bush, totally defeated and in sore need of something to soothe his pride…and his headache.

From a safe distance, hiding in the bushes, Hare watched the events at the river's edge with a great deal of interest. "Hmmm. It looks very much to me as if they are going about this in quite the wrong way." A plan began to form in his mind. After a while he hopped off into the bush and went home to work out the details.

Early next morning, Hare arrived at the old black tree as the river rolled quietly and peacefully by. Hare brought with him a goat, a dog, some vine and two wooden stakes. He was also carrying two bags; one containing meat and bones, and the other some freshly cut grass. Hare drove the two stakes into the ground some distance apart but near to the tree. Using the vine, he tied the dog to one of the stakes and the goat to the other. Next, he placed the grass in front of the dog and the meat in front of the goat. The vine that tied the dog to the stake was too short to allow it to reach the meat, nor was the goat able to reach the grass. Soon the animals became hungry. The dog started to bark and the goat set up a loud bleating.

Deep inside the tree, safe in his home, the otter was watching. He shook his head at Hare's stupidity. Surely everyone knows that dogs do not eat grass and goats do not eat meat? Finally, Kala the otter could stand it no longer. He jumped from his hole in the tree and gave the grass to the goat and the meat to the dog. But the woman and her daughter had been waiting. Before the otter could dash back to the safety of his home, the two women grabbed him. Hopping up, Hare reminded the old woman of their agreement. She was only too pleased to have her daughter marry Hare, who had proven himself to be the cleverest creature in all the land.

As far as I know, the big black tree still stands on the riverbank, although no-one lives in it now.

The March of the Hermit Crabs in the Rain

By Ashley Saunders

How wonderful,
yet how strange,
to see hermit crabs
marching in the rain.

For months they've lived
beneath the rocks
waiting for the sound
of those wondrous drops.

Then suddenly from under
their covers they proceed
with a hermit crab in a whelk shell
firmly in the lead

and thousands more following.
Their destination no one can tell;
it seems they only want to get wet
and display their shells

that they found washed upon the shore
along with the seaweed and driftwood
which they simply ignore.
Though to some hermit crabs

finding a shell that fits isn't
always that easy in life;
sometimes one has to settle for
a perfume bottle cap or an old clay pipe.

But what does it matter?
To hermit crabs it's all the same –
they only want a chance to march
in the rain.

Nkalimeva

Retold by Tom Nevin (Abridged)

The elephant was a good-natured and kindly animal. He was very big, and because of his size he was very clumsy. Not that the other animals were much bothered by this, although they became annoyed when he kept knocking things over. They understood this was because of his great size and made allowances for him.

But the elephant had another problem which was to be his downfall: he was very, very inquisitive. He just had to know everything that was going on. If he saw two animals having a conversation, he would trot over to hear what they were talking about. Because of his great size and height, he sometimes had to bend over to hear clearly what was being said.

Late one afternoon the elephant was walking down a path through the bush to the water hole. It was the time when the animals gathered for their daily drink and as usual there would be plenty of gossip. As he was passing a clump of low bushes, elephant heard the sound of voices coming from within. It was just a low murmur, just enough to catch his attention and stir his great curiosity. The elephant stopped in his tracks and looked down at the bushes, pricking his small ears so that he could hear more clearly what was being said.

Suddenly, the branches were whipped aside. The elephant came face to face with the most terrifying, most horrible creature he had ever seen. Nkalimeva! The little beast seemed to be all jaws, filled with wickedly long pointed teeth. When it spoke it was with a voice that rasped and growled, sending shivers of ice down the terrified elephant's back. "So," hissed Nkalimeva, "the elephant wants to know Nkalimeva's business, does he? The elephant is curious about what Nkalimeva is saying?"

"Oh, no! No, no. I was… I was just passing by. On my way to the w-water hole…" the frightened elephant stammered.

"You're lying to me, elephant!"

"No, no!" squealed the elephant. "I'm not. Truly, I'm not."

The horrible little creature stared at the elephant. His eyes glittered yellow and evil, his fangs gleamed white. Then he spoke again with low, fierce, growling words. "So elephant likes to poke his nose into other people's business. Elephant is so curious that he must know all that is going on, even though it does not concern him."

The elephant could only stare at Nkalimeva. He could not speak. No words would come.

"How can you poke your nose into other people's business when it is so small? That must be a problem for you, elephant."

Nkalimeva reached out his claw-like hand and grasped the elephant's nose firmly in his black nails. Elephant squealed with fright and tried to pull away. He tugged and twisted his head and wrenched his body from side to side, but Nkalimeva's grip on his nose was tight.

The great beast struggled to get free and at last began to make some ground. Little by little he moved backwards and then, at last, he was free! It happened so suddenly that he stumbled backwards and sat down with a hard 'thump' onto his great backside.

Elephant drew in a great breath of relief. But what was this? When he sucked in air, there was a great sound of whistling and snorting, like the wind through the reeds on the riverbed. Looking down he saw, dangling from his face, the longest strangest nose anyone had ever seen! It was long and thick and round. It was so big it was like the trunk of a small tree! Yes, it was a trunk.

"Now, Mr. Elephant," said Nkalimeva spitefully, "now you have the right nose to poke into everyone's business." He gave a loud cackle of laughter.

Sadly, the elephant turned to go away.

"Not so fast," hissed the ugly little beast. "I haven't finished with you yet." Reaching out his claws yet again, he grabbed the elephant's small ears, one in each hand. "We must make sure that you can hear everything that is being said, must we not? These ears are far too small."

Again there was a great tussle as the elephant tried to free his ears from Nkalimeva's iron grip. Although he shook his great head this way and that, there was no releasing his ears from the fierce little creature's grasp. Finally he stopped struggling and Nkalimeva let go. Elephant's ears were now so big, like the leaves of a banana tree, that he could even see them himself.

"Now, be on your way," growled Nkalimeva, "and let everyone see and be warned that the elephant has a nose for everyone's affairs and the ears to hear what everyone is saying."

With a heavy tread and an even heavier heart, the elephant walked off into the bush. To this very day he carries the burden that Nkalimeva gave him.

Black Noddy

By Makerita Vaai

before the sun is up
you abandon your perch
and head down towards the ocean
riding numerous waves
flying tirelessly
seeking food.

as the sun goes down
you return to your nest
lured by mating calls
faked on cassette
you swoop down unknowingly
ignorant of
being trapped
a victim
in the catcher's net.

Clever Tortoise

Retold by Francesca Martin (Abridged)

isten! There is a lake in Africa, called Nyasa. *Mmm*, it is full of blue cool water. On the banks of Nyasa live Rabbit, Warthog, Lizard, Hippopotamus, Snake, Elephant, *Chungu* – the little black ant – and many other animals. Clever Tortoise lives there too. See? Everyone is happy now. But once there was a quarrel. *Hmm, tch, tch*, it started like this…

"See how big I am?" cried Elephant one day. "I am stronger than all you little animals!" And a great big elephant-sized crashing and trampling and spoiling and stamping began in the bush by Lake Nyasa. *Och, tch, tch*, it was bad. *Hmm*, and it was catching.

"See how huge I am?" cried Hippopotamus another day. "I am stronger than all you small animals!" And a great huge hippopotamus-sized splashing and bubbling and churning started in the waters of Lake Nyasa. *Aah, tch, tch!* It was worse.

Rabbit, Snake, Lizard and the others grew frightened. Warthog called a meeting.

"What shall we do?" he said. "That elephant and that Hippopotamus are bullies." All the animals thought. Clever Tortoise thought too. *Ahh!* that tortoise. His head is small, but his brains are big and strong.

"Ha!" he said, after just a little time. "Let's play a trick on them…"

Pitter-patter, pitter-patter. Clever Tortoise led the others through the bush to find Elephant.

"Mr Mighty Elephant," Clever Tortoise called. "I hear you are the strongest. Will you fight a tug-of-war with me?"

"You?" snorted Elephant. "A little teeny tortoise? Fight a tug-of-war with ME!"

"Yes," said Clever Tortoise. "I will meet you right here at sun-up tomorrow, with a rope."

Pitter-patter, *pitter-patter*. Then Clever Tortoise took the others to the water to find Hippopotamus.

"Mrs Fine Hippopotamus," Clever Tortoise said. "I hear you are the strongest. Will you fight a tug-of-war with me?"

"You?" scoffed Hippopotamus. "A weeny small tortoise? Fight a tug-of-war with ME!"

"Yes," said Clever Tortoise. "I will meet you right here at sun-up tomorrow, with a rope."

That night, Clever Tortoise, Rabbit, Warthog, Lizard and the others stayed awake. *My!* What rustling and tying, what rolling and twisting, what knotting and plaiting of long strong tree vines there was – all through star-time – to weave one long strong rope. *Ha!* The sun rose, and the blue cool water of Lake Nyasa turned to red and gold. Elephant rose too.

"Good morning, Mr Elephant," Clever Tortoise said. "Will you take this end of our tug-of-war rope? Then we can begin."

"Huh!" snorted Elephant. "I will pull you over quicker than a hummingbird beats its wings!"

But where do you think Clever Tortoise and his friends went with the other end of their long strong rope? *Ha!*

"Good morning, Mrs Hippopotamus," Clever Tortoise said. "Will you take this end of our tug-of-war rope? Then we can begin."

"Humph!" snorted Hippopotamus. "I will pull you over faster than a frog can jump!"

But that boasty Hippopotamus and that proud Elephant, they had one enormous surprise coming their way…

"NGGHHHHH!" grunted Elephant.

"MMMMMPH!" groaned Hippopotamus, as the tug of war began.

"OOOOOOOF!" moaned Elephant.

"AI-AI!" gasped Hippopotamus, as the tug-of-war went on.

And each of them thought, "This tincy tortoise, he is very strangely STRONG."

The sun climbed high and higher in the sky, till there was not one shadow left in all Africa. *Ooh*, and it was hot. But still the rope stayed tight.

"Enough!" said Clever Tortoise. And he cut the rope with a little stone axe. Well, what do you think happened then? CRASH! fell Elephant, and he bumped his big strong head. SPLASH! fell Hippopotamus, and she smacked her broad great back.

Pitter-patter, pitter-patter. Clever Tortoise went to visit Elephant in the bush.

"Quicker than a hummingbird beats its wings?" he called. Elephant just stared at that teeny tortoise. Where did he hide his strength? In his toes?

Pitter-patter, pitter-patter. Clever Tortoise went to visit Hippopotamus by the water.

"Faster than a frog can jump?" he called. Hippopotamus just gazed at that weeny tortoise. Where did he hide his strength? Underneath his shell?

That night, Elephant and Hippopotamus slept a deep tired tug-of-war sleep. But the smaller animals stayed awake. **My!** What clapping and swinging, what dancing and jumping, happened in the moonlight!

"You clever, Clever Tortoise!" cheered Rabbit, Warthog, Lizard, Snake, *Chungu* – the little black ant – and all the others. "That was one good trick!"

And that's how that quarrel was mended. See? All the animals are happy again. *Kwa heri ya kuonana, wanangu* – so long, children, till we meet again.

WAVES
UPON THE
SHORE

When it's Summer

By Roma Potiki

when it's summer
and earth and sky almost meet
i lie down, stomach-up on the sand dunes

bare skin
and sun
and the sea lifting
and pressing down on sand.

and even though my eyes are closed i feel the imprint of the
season
the wash of light and heat on my lids

relaxing
i breathe in the saline breath of Tangaroa
smell the pumice and earth mingling.

and it's all sensation
as i stand and run down to the sea, to the water.
feel its kick and rhythm
its fish music.

buoyant and strong i am carried back
to the lip of firm sand.

foam loops over my ankles
i smile and dig my hands in.

Kader

Adapted from a retelling by Meredic Adrienne

here was a man called Kader. One day the king said to him, "Kader, go to the sun and ask why he rises red and sets red." Kader went.

Passing by the seaside, he met a little karang fish washed up on the beach. Kader put it back in the sea, and the fish said, "Thank you, Kader! When you need my services, I'll be there."

Kader said, "But you're a fish in the sea! How can you do any service for me?"

Kader went on his way.

As he passed through the forest, the breeze was so strong that a young blackbird fell out of the nest, so Kader picked it up and put it back. The father and mother blackbird were very happy, and said to him that some day they would pay him back. But again Kader didn't believe that.

When Kader reached the sun's place, three-quarters of its rays had disappeared over the horizon. Kader called out to him.

The sun said, "Who is calling me?"

Kader said, "It's me, Kader. The king sent me to ask why you come up red and why you set red."

So the sun said to Kader, "Tell the king to go to church, and the priest will tell him why I rise red and set red. Tell him to work on Sundays to pay his debts, and that there's a queen of the fish who is more beautiful than his dead wife."

Kader thanked the sun and began his journey home.

Finally he reached the king's palace and told him what the sun had said. Well, the king was very happy! He said to Kader, "I want you to go and find me that queen of the fish."

So Kader took his little boat, hauled the anchor, and rowed out to sea. He met a karang fish. The karang said, "Kader! Don't you recognise me?" The karang had grown up by then. "You're the one who saved my life when the waves washed me up on the beach. What are you doing?"

So Kader said to him, "I'm looking for the queen of the fish. The king sent me to find her."

The fish said, "Don't worry, I'll go and get her for you." So the karang brought the queen of the fish and Kader took her to the king's palace. Oh, the king was happy. The queen was pretty! Her hair went down to her hips. Her eyes were blue! No joke! She was really beautiful, the queen of the fish! The king could do nothing but kiss her.

Years passed and the king became old. So he said to Kader, "Kader, go and find me a potion somewhere to make me young again."

Kader said, "Oh king, where am I going to find that elixir?"

The king said, "Walk, walk, maybe you'll find someone who'll be able to give you that little remedy."

So Kader set out.

Walking along he met a male and female blackbird but Kader didn't recognise them. The father blackbird said, "When our child fell out of the nest and fell to the ground, you picked her up and put her back in the nest. You did us a great service, so we will do you any service you like!"

Kader said, "The king has told me to fetch a potion to make him young again."

So the two blackbirds took a little bottle and flew towards the sky. Around the middle of the next day, they came back to Kader. The female said to Kader, "Take this water and give it to the king. He'll drink from it and he'll become young again."

The male said to him, "Take this water and keep it with you. Maybe some day you'll need it."

Kader thanked them and left.

The king meanwhile was waiting impatiently for him. When Kader came back, the king was very happy. He drank the mother blackbird's water and he became young again. Ah, the king was very handsome! The queen too was very happy. She clasped him around the neck and kissed him.

But youth does not last forever. Several years passed and the king noticed that he was again getting old. He said to Kader, "Don't you see me getting old again?"

Kader said, "Oh yes, my king. I'll go."

He went and got the remedy the male blackbird had given him, and gave it to the king. The king drank that water and a few days later he was dead.

So Kader inherited the king's town and married the queen of the fish.

One day, I was passing by and said, "What do you say, Kader? You got you a beautiful wife!" Kader didn't like that! He gave me a kick, and I fell here.

Dawn is a Fisherman

By Raymond Barrow

Dawn is a fisherman, his harpoon of light
Poised for a throw – so swiftly morning comes:
The darkness squats upon the sleeping land
Like a flung cast-net, and the black shapes of boats
Lie hunched like nesting turtles
On the flat calm of the sea.

Among the trees the houses peep at the stars
Blinking farewell, and half-awakened birds
Hurtle across the vista, some in the distance
Giving their voice self-criticised auditions.

Warning comes from the cocks, their necks distended
Like city trumpeters: and suddenly
Between the straggling fences of grey cloud
The sun, a barefoot boy, strides briskly up
The curved beach of the sky, flinging his greetings
Warmly in all directions, laughingly saying
Up, up, the day is here! Another day is here!

The Two Crabs

Adapted from a retelling by Manel Ratnatunga

It is said that once in a certain country there lived a crab with her little son.

One beautiful sunny morning, the crab and her son went for a long stroll on the beach by the sea. The crashing waves made lovely music in their ears. The palm trees waved to and fro in the breeze. There were a lot of happy people sitting under the palms and watching the scene.

The crab mother became self-conscious. So many people were watching her and her son taking a walk on the beach. She looked at her son and was horrified to see the way he walked.

"Son," she said sternly, "why do you waddle sideways when you walk? You look so funny, so graceless. And all these people watching! Learn to walk straight without going crookedly."

The little crab was deeply hurt. He retorted at once, "Well, mother, I was only copying you. I thought it was the way to walk since that is the way you walk. If my walk is not nice, walk straight yourself first and I will do as you do. Show me how to do it."

The crab mother was silenced.

"You are right, my son," she said at last. "I can do no better."

So the two crabs continued to walk crookedly down the beach on that beautiful sunny morning.

The Sea is a Mystery

By Kay Polydore

The sea to me is always a mystery.
One day, it is an expanse of serenity,
A giant light blue mirror
That seems knitted to the sky.
Then it is a mere inanimate thing.
When the breeze stirs its body,
It resembles crinkly crepe.
On certain days some devil teases it
And it roars like a hungry lion,
Terrifying sailors and landlubbers,
Pounding the shore with gigantic breakers,
Thus excavating the beach
And restructuring the coastline.
At such times it seems to be a living being,
Intent solely on destruction.
Another puzzle is who or what
Colours its waters?
Powder blue, aquamarine,
Turquoise, peppermint, navy-blue,
The colours change with its mood.
It dons an iron-grey attire
Or one of leaden blue
When it is angry and intent
On scaring with its evil look.
Who pacifies and controls it?
This remains a mystery to me.

Seashell

By James Berry

Seashell at my ear –
come share how I hear
busy old sea in whispers.

Moans rise from ancient depths
in ocean sighs
like crowds of ghost monsters.

Waves lash and fall –
in roars and squalls
with all a mystery ahhh!

Citronella

By Carl De Souza

nce upon a time, there lived a little girl called Citronella who could not hear. She could not hear what her father told her. She could not hear her mother's good advice. She could not hear what her brothers and sisters said.

"This child must be deaf," said her aunt one day.

Everyone agreed with her. They decided that Citronella should see the local doctor. He was not a very good doctor, but he was the only one in that part of the country.

"Can you hear me?" asked the doctor while he listened with his stethoscope.

"What?" asked Citronella.

"This little girl is deaf," he confirmed.

The doctor prescribed drops for her ears and pills that she had to take before meals. "This medicine should make her hear properly," the doctor told her family.

"Yes, yes!" shouted everybody – except little Citronella, who said "What?"

The eardrops tickled her ears. The pills tasted like bitter leaves. After a while, it became clear that they weren't helping. Citronella could still not hear anything she was told.

The family was losing hope. They decided to take Citronella to see Bilimbi. Bilimbi was a healer who had magical powers. Everyone feared him.

As soon as he saw Citronella, he said "Someone has cast a spell on this child. She can't hear because bad spirits are eating up the sounds in her ears." He told the family to grind up the shells of some big snails and to sprinkle the powder on her head. "Then paint her nose with the droppings of a bird that eats only fruit," he said. "Oh, I almost forgot. She should also hold a lighted red candle," he added.

The family obeyed all of Bilimbi's orders. They ground the shells of some big snails and sprinkled the powder on Citronella's head. They put fresh bird droppings on her nose. Yuk! She sat there, holding her breath, with a lighted red candle in her hand.

Then her brothers and sisters asked her loudly, "Citronella, can you hear us?"

"What?" asked Citronella.

People thought she really didn't *want* to hear them, so they no longer bothered with Citronella.

They sent Citronella to her grandfather, Tambala. He was very, very old. He too had been unable to hear anything for a long time. Grandpa Tambala sat quietly in his armchair. He said nothing, not a single word. He just looked at Citronella for a long time, without blinking. Then he smiled. Finally, he struggled to his feet, took Citronella's hand and they left the house together.

They walked along a path, with hedges on both sides, which led to a sugar cane field. Freshly harvested sugar cane lay tied in bundles along the path. The wind blew the sweet smell towards them. The sun shone down. They wandered along the furrows. Little Citronella could feel the grasses brush against her ankles and the crunch of soil under her feet. She could feel the breeze in her hair and the heat of the sun on her cheeks. She saw the clouds move slowly across the sky, and the birds in the thorn bushes. Grandpa Tambala and Citronella followed the gentle curves of the path towards the beach. They could feel the rustling of the wings of the dragonfly and the flapping of the palm branches in the breeze. Waves lapped gently on the shore.

There, at last, they stopped, staring at the ocean with the sound of their breathing in their ears.

It began to get dark. Grandpa Tambala sat down against the rocks. Citronella lay with her head on his chest, listening to his old heart beating: *togodok-togodok-togodok*.

The search party found them there early the next morning, after spending the whole night looking for them. Grandpa Tambala's eyes were still closed. Citronella, who was sitting beside him, saw her father, her mother, her aunt, her brothers and sisters, the doctor and Bilimbi in a big crowd, running towards them.

"There they are! We have found them. Little Citronella and Tambala, the old man!" they shouted.

Citronella jumped up and stood in the middle of the path, red with anger. She put her finger to her lips and said "Shhh!" She pointed to the sleeping old man.

They stopped shouting. They stopped crying. Everyone was silent, so that they would not wake up old Tambala.

For the first time, the people could hear the babbling of the water, the song of the wind in the trees, and the clicking of the crabs' claws. They stood still and looked at little Citronella. They were sorry for the way they had treated her. For a long time, they stood there, listening.

And they realised that they had not been listening properly for a long time. There were things to be heard that you could not hear with your ears.

Tambala, the old man, never woke up. They dug a big bed for him in the fine beach sand. Now he could never be far from the songs of the fish. They left him there to rest in peace.

Citronella returned home with the others. She carried the memory of Grandpa Tambala in her head – the *togodok* of his heart would be with her always. She knew that she had heard the *togodok* sound. No one could convince her that she could not hear.

And she was sure of one thing: from now on, she would be able to make her father, her mother, and all the others hear what she had to say.

THE SALTY
SEA BREEZE

The Legend of the Golden Apple Tree

By *Timothy Callender* (Adapted Extract)

ow there was a tree on a small plantation in St. Victoria. This one tree surprised everybody. It grow tall and strong, reaching up in the sky so far that people wonder when it going stop growing, and what kind of tree it was. Then one year the tree put out some tiny flowers, and the bees come around it, buzzing like busybodies. Sunlight twinkle off the tree, and it seem to give off a glow. Everybody shake their head and say, "This is a wonderful tree. I wonder what kind of fruit it will bear."

Then little fruits appear on this tree, green at first, then starting to turn yellow. By and by, the whole tree was covered with plenty yellow fruit, about as big as a boy's fist. The birds loved the fruit. The islanders see that the tree was good for food. They come from all over the island to buy fruit from St. Victoria. They name the fruit golden-apples.

One morning an islander named John Ibo decide he go leave the island. He jump-in a rowboat and head out to sea. After three days a ship pick him up. But he was worse off than before, because it was a pirate ship.

Ibo start feeling real fed-up. You would feel fed-up, too, if you find yuhself on a pirate ship. Pirates don't cool-out. When they ain't drinking rum, they fighting. When they ain't drinking rum and fighting, they planning to burn a city, or sink somebody ship, or search for gold. That is the worse part, when pirates start searching for gold. When pirates hear about gold, their eyes does light up. They does ask where it is, and who got it, and how to get to the place where the gold is, and how to thief the gold, or fight the people who got the gold. Pirates ain't got no conscience. I very sorry to say. When they hear the word gold, their sense does fly out the window. And they would believe anything they hear 'bout gold. Every minute they talking about it.

Well, it seem that Ibo tek-in sick; he can't even remember exactly what happen, but all he know is that he lay down and next minute, it seemed, he opened his eyes, and every pirate on board that ship was there looking down at him. "Wake up!" they shouting at him. "We don't want you dead. You got to live, man."

Ibo can't understand why it is, all of a sudden, everybody so concerned about his health. He looking around confused.

One man begin to explain. "Listen, fellow, you have bin sick. You were delirious for a week. You talked about a lot of things. You talked about the Island of Barbados, and about the plantation of St. Victoria, and about a tree that's growing there…"

At this point the Captain say, "Shut up! Another word, and I'll have ye put in chains!" Then he motion to the mate and the bo'son, and tell them to bring Ibo to his cabin.

Now Captain William was the worst captain in the then-known world. He didn't have no respect, and he didn't get no respect. He know he living on borrowed time. He know night does run till daylight catch it. He know that the longest day got an ending, that time longer than rope but shorter than elastic, and that the sand in the hour-glass going soon run out.

The Captain look at Ibo. The Captain parrot look at Ibo, too. Both the parrot and the Captain cock their head and stare at Ibo with one bright eye.

The Captain growl: "I want some information. I have heard of this legend of a tree that grows apples of gold, on the Island of Barbados. You have seen this tree?"

"Ah – yes – sir. But, yuh see…"

"So it is true! Such a tree really exists! Why, this is better than the goose that laid the golden egg. Is it a big tree? Does it bear once a year?"

"But sir, these apples – yuh see, sir, these apples…"

"This is enough. We will go to Barbados. You will take me to this tree. Imagine! Apples of Gold!"

"But sir, a golden-apple tree and a tree with apples of gold is not…"

"Do you question what I say?"

"Er – no sir."

"Good. I am tired of sailing the seas. Time for me to settle down, and farm golden apples."

"Right sir, anything you say." Ibo ain't saying nothing more, he only glad that they headed Barbados-way.

The Captain laughed. "When I get to Barbados, I am going to…"

"To the hangman noose! To the hangman noose!" the parrot call out.

Well the Captain give orders to head for Barbados, and all the time he sailing there, he smiling to heself. They stop the ship far out by the horizon, and the Captain and Ibo get into the life-boat and start for the shore. Long before they reach the plantation, they see the tree of golden apples. Sun shining down, and the tree twinkling and glowing, one spectacular sight.

Then the Captain gone wild. He hurry forward leaving Ibo behind. Ibo frightened; he wondering what the man going do when he discover that the golden apples was a kind of fruit. But Ibo wasn't a fool. He send somebody to call the militia quick-quick.

By the time Ibo get to the golden-apple tree, the Captain was sitting down crying, and holding one golden-apple in his hand. Ibo can't see why the Captain carrying on so. True, he disappointed, but still… Then the Captain raise he head and point out to sea, and Ibo see that the ship was slipping away, sneaking off over the horizon. The crew was tekking it and leaving the Captain behind. The Captain didn't have neither gold nor golden apples now.

The parrot turn out to be right: the Captain went to the hangman noose, and that was the end of his singular career.

Once the Wind

By Shake Keane

Once the wind
said to the sea
I am sad
    And the sea said
Why
    And the wind said
Because I
am not blue like the sky
or like you

    So the sea said what's
so sad about that
        Lots
of things are blue
or red or other colours too
    but nothing
neither sea nor sky
can blow so strong
or sing so long as you

    And the sea looked sad
        So the wind said
Why

Si Perawai, the Greedy Fisherman

Adapted from a retelling by Margaret Read MacDonald

It was just an ordinary day to begin with. Si Perawai threw out his long fishing line, then pulled it in. Threw out his long line, then pulled it in. All day he had been working like this. But each time he pulled in the line, there was not one fish on it.

It was getting late in the afternoon, when suddenly he saw all of the floats on his line start to jiggle. Something was on the line! Quickly he started to haul in his catch. But when he pulled the line in, he found that caught on the end of his line was a long chain. At first he thought to toss it back overboard, but then as he looked at it closer he saw a gleam from beneath the sea scum. He rubbed at the chain. OH MY! The chain was solid gold!

Si Perawai held tight to the chain. Its end was still dragging in the water. Perhaps it was longer. Who knew how long?

Si Perawai began to pull the chain's length into the boat. "I can sell this gold chain!" he thought. "I will be able to buy a new net, and new fishing lines!"

Then, as he realised that the chain was longer than he had at first thought, his dreams began to grow. "I will be able to buy a new boat!"

Still the chain did not end. Si Perawai was ecstatic. "I will be able to build a new house!" he exclaimed as he hauled in more and more of the golden chain.

The heavy chain was piling up in the boat, coiling round and round, heavier and heavier.

"I will be able to buy more land! I will have new clothing!" thought the crazed Si Perawai.

The boat was sinking lower and lower in the water.

"I will throw a feast! I will be famous!"

Hand over hand, he hauled in more and more of the heavy golden chain.

Now the boat had sunk completely into the sea, and the water was ready to pour into his boat.

"I will…" With a great swoosh, the boat sank beneath the waves with Si Perawai and the yards and yards of golden chain.

Sailing Under Moonlit Skies

By Farah Didi

let us sail on a sunset sky,
feel the wind against our hair,
let us savour the spray
that soaks our faces,
let us glide across endless horizons,
into a moonlit night,
let us set sail on the dying sun,
and wait for the moon to arise,
flooding the sea
with silver lights,
above a million stars,
winking at our grateful hearts.

let us rig up a lively jib,
against the rising breeze,
caress the hungry sails,
and drift across dancing waves,
feel the rising rhythm in our souls,
sometimes a samba, sometimes a waltz,
sometimes silence, nothing at all,
let us set sail and dream away,
let our souls, our thoughts, and minds
fly free across a silvery bay,
let us be content
in a moonlit heaven,
let us go sailing by.

The Three Brothers

Retold by Jan Knappert (Abridged)

Once upon a time there was a sultan who had three sons. When the eldest came of age, he begged his father for a ship. His father consented and had a beautiful sailing vessel built for him. Then away he sailed to distant India, across the glittering ocean.

Shortly afterwards the second son had the same request, which was likewise granted, and finally the third and youngest son was allowed to sail out on the splendid waves towards the golden sands of India.

The eldest landed on a lonely beach where he met an old woman who wanted him to buy a basket: "Think, prince, this basket not only carries your bread, it also carries your body, as it can fly in no time through the air!"

The prince agreed to buy the basket.

The second son of the sultan also landed on that beach, a little while later. While he was exploring that strange country, he too met the old lady. She persuaded him to buy an old ornamental mirror: "Greetings, grandson! This mirror will show you any place or person on earth that you want. Just look and you will see many lovely things!"

The young prince looked into the mirror but he did not see himself. Instead, he saw his parents sitting in their palace. After a moment, that image disappeared and the prince saw a beautiful girl who was bathing in a pond. Just then she looked up and smiled. The prince felt his heart jump and fell hopelessly in love with that picture. He bought the mirror for a high price and continued his voyage, all the time thinking about the beautiful bather whose every movement he followed in his mirror, simply by wishing to see her.

The third son, likewise, landed on the lonely beach, but one of his sailors, who wanted to explore the forest, was caught by a tiger and killed. At that moment, while he was alone in the forest, he met the old woman who addressed him thus: "Greetings, prince, your servant died but my powder can make him live again! Buy this bag with the powder of life and you will be happy! Let me show you how to use it."

The woman knelt down near the dead sailor and strewed some powder into the wounds that the tiger's claws had left. After a few moments the body began to stir, the eyes opened and life returned. The sailor stood up and greeted his master. The prince was overjoyed and paid a high price for the miraculous powder. After this they said farewell to the mysterious old woman and boarded their ship.

Not long afterwards, the three brothers met together in a great port city and related to each other their adventures. The second son found out that it was in that city that the girl lived whom he had been watching in his magic mirror all the time. It appeared that she was the daughter of the sultan of that city, and together the three princes called at the palace and asked to see her.

Alas! The king received them with cries of sorrow. That morning a demon had swooped down from the sky and caught the princess while she was bathing. With his royal prey he had flown away on his black wings, to where – no one knew.

The second prince looked in his mirror: he saw the princess lying dead in the middle of a forest. The first prince took his basket, sat in it, and flew to the forest. There he found the princess, took her in his basket, and flew back to the palace. Now the third prince knelt near the poor dead princess and began to scatter his powder over her face and body. Soon she began to blink her eyes, and finally rose up and embraced her parents.

At once each of the three princes claimed her for himself.

"I brought her here from the forest," said the eldest. "Without me she would still be lying there in that lonely place."

"I could see where she was," the second prince said. "Without my mirror you could not even have known that she existed."

"Without my magic medicine she would still be dead and no one could have married her," the third prince protested.

The three sultan's sons quarrelled on until they finally came to an agreement. They would go and find the mysterious woman on the beach and ask her to solve their dilemma. This was done!

The princes set sail and landed on the lonely beach. The old woman appeared and seemed to know their problem.

"He who carried her in his arms acted as her father," she said. "He who brought her back to life is her guardian and healer. But he who fell in love with her when he saw her bathing, stayed faithful to her and thought of her day and night, he will be her husband."

At that, she vanished. The eldest brother took his basket and flew back to his father's country where he was crowned king in the course of time. The second son married the princess he loved and became king in her father's kingdom. The third prince received the fleet with all its wealth and travelled round, curing the sick so that he became a famous doctor.

We Have Come Home

By Lenrie Peters *(An Extract)*

We have come home
To the green foothills
To drink from the cry
Of warm and mellow birdsong.
To the hot beaches
Where boats go out to sea
Threshing the ocean's harvest
And the harassing, plunging,
gliding gulls shower kisses on the waves.

Rajah Suran's Expedition to China

Retold by Sheila Wee (Abridged)

nce in the time long ago, there was a king. His name was Rajah Suran, and he ruled over India. But India wasn't enough for him. He wanted to be the most powerful king in the world. He made all the princes of the nearby countries bow down to him, pay him taxes of rice and gold, and call him the most powerful king.

Still he wasn't happy. There was someone who refused to say that he was the greatest king, and that was the Emperor of China. This made Rajah Suran very angry, and he decided he would invade China. He gathered a huge army with soldiers from every part of his empire.

But Rajah Suran had a problem. You see, he wasn't exactly sure where China was. He thought that it was in the south, so he led his army into Burma and followed the coast southward. Down through Burma they went and into Thailand, then further south into Malaysia. They kept on marching for month after month, until at last they reached the beaches of the Straits of Johor and stood looking across the water to the island of Singapore. Though in those long ago times it was not called Singapore; it was called Temasek.

There they had to stop and build rafts to ferry them across the water. This took some time, but at last the whole army was assembled on the north shore of Temasek. Rajah Suran gave the order to march southward, but it didn't take long before they reached the Southern Sea and could go no farther. Rajah Suran realised that if he wanted to reach China he would now have to travel by sea. So he set his men to building hundreds of strong ships. But he still didn't know which way to go, so he also sent men off in every direction with instructions to find the way to China and find it quickly.

Now, Rajah Suran's journey to Temasek had not been a secret, could not have been a secret, not with so many men, horses, and elephants making the ground thunder with their footsteps. Traders who sailed the coast trading in gold, spices and aromatic wood heard of Rajah Suran's plan, and they told their friends about the huge army that was looking for the way to China. Now their friends told their friends and their friends told their friends and their friends told their friends, until eventually someone told the Emperor of China himself.

The Emperor was very worried. He called his ministers together and asked their advice. "What shall we do? If Rajah Suran finds the way to our land, he will surely defeat us; his army is so much bigger, so much stronger than ours. We must find a way to stop him."

The Emperor and his ministers sat down to think. They thought all day and they thought all night, and then just as the dawn was breaking, the Chief Minister burst out laughing.

"Oh yes, I have it, I have a very good plan," he cried. He whispered his plan into the Emperor's ears and the Emperor smiled for the first time in days.

"Yes, that is a very good plan; go and get the things you need at once."

And so the Chief Minister went down to the harbour to find a ship to sail to Temasek, to sail to Singapore. But he didn't look for the best ship, the fastest ship, the newest ship. No, he searched the harbour until he found the oldest ship there was. Its planks were worn and its sails were yellow with age. The Chief Minister chose the sailors himself. He chose the oldest men he could find. Some of them were so old they could hardly walk and had to be carried onto the ship.

"Old men, sailing an old ship; the Chief Minister's gone crazy," the people said.

Then the Chief Minister did something that seemed just as ridiculous: he ordered that huge fruit trees should be dug up, planted in pots, and carried

on board the ship. Last, he ordered that all the needles in the city should be brought to the palace. By the next morning the palace courtyard was filled with great piles of sewing needles. The Chief Minister ordered the servants to pick out all the old and rusty needles and put them into sacks. The servants worked hard, and by nightfall they had gathered fifty sacks full of rusty needles.

Everyone wondered, "An old ship with old sailors, old fruit trees, and old rusty needles; how is that going to save us from the terrible army of Rajah Suran?"

The Emperor and the Chief Minister heard what people were saying, but they did not say a word, they just smiled as they waved the ship off on its journey.

A few weeks later the ship arrived in Temasek. Rajah Suran and all his men were still there, and they still didn't know the way to China. When the lookouts spotted the old ship limping into the harbour, with huge fruit trees growing on its deck and a crew of old grandfathers, they couldn't stop laughing. Soon everyone had heard about the strange ship, and even Rajah Suran himself came to take a look.

"Where have you come from?" he asked. "What country is it that has such old sailors?"

The oldest of the sailors spoke up, "We have come from China. When we set out we were all strong young men – we were carrying a cargo of fruit tree seeds and iron bars. But it took us so long to get here that we have grown old, the seeds have become trees, and the iron bars have rusted away to the size of needles." And he opened one of the sacks of needles to show Rajah Suran.

Rajah Suran looked down and sighed. If China was that far away, he would be an old man before they got there, and his soldiers would be old also – too old to fight. No, it was not worth it; he would send his army back to India and find some other, nearer land to conquer.

And so the huge army turned around and marched back the way it had come and China was saved.

Sun, Moon and the Starry Sky

The Messenger of the Moon

Adapted from a retelling by Mervyn Skipper

There was a drought in the Elephant country. There hadn't been a drop of rain for weeks. All the pools and the lakes had dried up, and instead of a beautiful broad river to bathe in, all the elephants had was a little muddy trickle of water which was hardly enough to give them each a drink, not to speak of a bath.

So the King of the Elephants sent a messenger out to see if, in another part of the country, there was any water to be found. The messenger travelled for many days over the hills and through the jungle, and everywhere he found the lakes had all dried up and the pools were all gone and the rivers were just little muddy trickles of water.

But at last, after many days of travelling, he came to a river where the grass was still green and the water was lovely and deep, and after drinking a little and giving himself a shower-bath, he hurried back to the King to tell him the good news. As soon as the King of the Elephants heard it, he told all his people to follow him, and set off to find the wonderful river.

Now the river belonged to a tribe of monkeys, and when some of the monkey people saw the elephants coming they went to their King and said, "What shall we do, O King? The elephant people are coming, like mountains walking, to take our river from us."

The Monkey King called all his people together and asked the oldest and wisest monkeys to tell him how he could stop the elephant people coming and drinking up their river. Some said one thing and some said another, but none of them could tell him how the elephant people could be stopped from drinking up their river.

At last a little baby monkey jumped up and said, "I will stop these elephants from stealing our beautiful river and drinking it all up."

The monkey people all laughed at him and cried, "How will you, a little whipper-snapper that a baby elephant could crush under one foot, stop a whole tribe of elephants?"

"That is my business," said the little monkey, "just you wait and see!"

So the little monkey went off and climbed a tree that leaned over the river and waited for the elephants. Soon they came along, hundreds of big old-man elephants and hundreds of big old-mother elephants and lots of little baby elephants who could have crushed the little monkey with one foot; and the ground shook under their tread, and the trees bent as if a strong wind were blowing, and all the leaves trembled. The little monkey did not tremble. He said in his squeaky voice, "Stop! Stop, all you elephant people! If you go another step further you will be sorry for it!"

The elephants all stopped and looked up, and when they saw a little monkey on a tree branch they laughed, and their King said, "Who are you, small hairy thing, that tells the elephant tribe to stop?"

"I am the messenger of the Moon, and the Moon owns all this river," said the little monkey. "There she is, bathing in it at this moment, and if you dare disturb her she will be very angry, and will certainly eat you all up!"

The elephants all looked at the river, and there, sure enough, was the Moon bathing in it.

So they all gathered at the bank of the river and talked about what was the best thing to do; some said one thing and some said another, but before they had made up their minds, a little baby elephant, trying to push his way to the front so that he could hear what his elders were talking about, fell, flop! into the river.

At once the Moon stopped bathing and began to rush up and down and round and round, as if she was terribly angry. The Elephant King, thinking he was going to be eaten, gave a wild scream and rushed away; and all the elephant tribe, the big old-man elephants and the big old-mother elephants and all the little baby elephants, rushed after him, falling over each other in their hurry.

The baby elephant who had fallen into the river pulled himself out as fast as he was able, and ran too. But after a while, noticing that the Moon wasn't following him, he stopped, and as he was very thirsty, he came tiptoeing back to the river, and there was the Moon, bathing herself quietly again. So he gently put his trunk into the water and took a little sip; and then, as the Moon did not seem to mind, he took a long gulp, and then he slipped down the bank, splosh! into the water and gave himself a shower-bath.

When he had had enough, he ran after the rest of the elephants to tell them that it was all right and that there was nothing to be afraid of. He had not gone very far when he met his mother, looking very pale and anxious. "You young rascal," she said, "wherever have you been? I was quite sure the Moon had caught and eaten you!"

"Caught and eaten me?" said the baby elephant, "No way! That Moon you were all so afraid of was only a reflection. I've just had a lovely shower-bath in her river, and if you all come back you can have one too!"

"Hold your tongue, you cheeky little thing, and come along," said the mother elephant, cuffing him over the head with her trunk, and hurrying to catch up with the rest.

So the elephant tribe went back to their own country and the monkey tribe kept their beautiful river.

How the Starfish got to the Sea

By Althea Trotman (Abridged)

De tale start one night when all de stars was shining in de sky. One bumptious star decide he coming down to de earth. So next ting you know, Brother Star just kafumkum down to de ground an' stop just so.

All de while, when Brother Star laying down, he saying to himself, "Ah going stay right here an' shine. Who say Ah must walk up an' down sky all night wid dem rest star? Ah going lie down right here-so an' smile. Look it have breeze to talk to an' all dem trees to laugh an' talk wid. Just lie down an' shine, nothing else to do."

Well, after a few days, when Brother Star just lying down an' smiling an' shining, he start to get dull. No shine coming 'tall, 'tall. He puff up him chest. Just like how you does see cock puff up him chest when he going crow, but still not a shine coming from Brother Star.

So Brother Star say, "Poor me, all me shine gone an' Ah is a star. How come me star-shine gone?"

Everybody did feel so sorry for poor Brother Star. But nobody did know how to help him.

Den a butterfly pass by. A pretty-pretty butterfly. She say to Brother Star, "How come you just lying down? How come you not shining when night come like dem rest star? Ent you used to walk 'cross sky every night an' light up de place?"

Brother Star answer her, "All of a sudden, me star-shine gone."

Sister Butterfly give him a saucy look an' say, "But no wonder you star-shine gone. 'Cause you just lying down an' smiling-smiling. How you going keep you star-shine if you not charging it up? How you tink dese wings so pretty-pretty? Is 'cause me flying from flower to flower. Else me sure dem would a drop off by now."

And so saying, Sister Butterfly do two turns round Brother Star head, her wings dem spread out pretty-pretty.

Poor Brother Star just lie down an' watch Sister Butterfly.

Now Brother Star wish he could go back up in de sky an' shine again. But how to do it? He never know what to do.

Donkey's years pass an' Brother Star still just lying down. One day, rain fall heavy-heavy. So heavy dat everyting start wash away to sea.

Poor Brother Star was frighten. 'Cause he couldn't hold his ground an' he didn't know how to swim. Remember, he don't have foot like you children an' he didn't have any fin like de fish of de sea.

All poor Brother Star could do was just lie down an' cry. His cry-water even mix up wid all de rain dat was falling.

De rain wash him all de way down de footpath over yonder. All de way down to de shore.

He met up some periwinkle on de sand an' dey feel so sorry for Brother Star dey stay all round him to keep him company. But dey couldn't hold him back from de sea when de big wave come. All dat rain did bring ground swell. An' one high-high wave just double him over.

Brother Star was sure he reach de end of his life. He was expecting to drown. Next ting he know, he feel as if he was floating. An' den he notice he have some little fin underneath his body dat open up an' start to move. He was swimming, just like if he was a fish!

He could not understand it a 'tall. He never go in sea in his life! An' he never see any fin on his body before. Den he look in de water an' he see his self. Well, he was so frighten!

He was brown an' pink, wid some little fin underneath his body. An' he see some bumps on his skin too. An' wait! De nice star body he used to have wasn't dere. Now he was a shell body! Only ting dat he find look de same was he still have a star shape.

So now all you know where starfish come from.

The Sun Witness

By Nurunnessa Choudhury

Long ago a young girl
wearing a saffron coloured saree
walked gracefully
on her way –
she moved the square stone
from the white
near-dead grass
by the lightening speed
of her black hand.

Silently, with her gaze,
she commanded the sun
to send its light
down upon everything,
even the white grass.

The sun accepted
her easy command
and came down with humility.

Days after,
she passed beggars in the street,
and tucked in her silk saree
to avoid their stains.

Seeing this,
the sun hid behind clouds,
and rain came,
unexpectedly, like tears.

Right Here Was the Ocean

By Zehra Nigah

Right here was the ocean,
angry, petulant,
pounding its head against the rocks,
growling, crashing and roaring,
boasting of its might and power;
the reticent, modest moon
in the sky,
its friend,
kept pace with it,
the ocean yearning
to hold the moon
in its arms.

Only a few signs remain,
all else is gone;
hunched and stooping rocks,
their parched tongues sticking out,
murky water, in patches
lining a barren shore,
but the friend is loyal still;
in the shriveling patches,
it can spot its image still.

The Moon in Swampland

Retold by M.P. Robertson (Abridged)

The stars were always telling the Moon about the dark deeds that went on in Swampland whenever her back was turned. One night she said, "I'll see for myself." She put on human form, and shrouding her silver hair in a cloak of night, she glided down to earth.

The Moon landed on a path winding between murky pools. The only light came from Will-o'-the-Wisps, who tried to lure her from the safety of the path with the eerie glow of their lanterns.

The Moon picked her way through the shadows. She saw vague shapes lurking in the mist. She heard horrible squelchings and evil belchings. When she wandered too close to the water's edge, clammy, webbed fingers snatched at her cloak.

The bogles were hungry tonight!

The Moon skipped lightly from stone to tussock until, tripping over a loose rock, she grabbed at a clump of reeds to steady herself. The reeds coiled around her wrists. She tugged and twisted, but the more she tugged, the tighter the reeds held her. As the Moon struggled, she heard the cry of a child. A boy had been led astray by Will-o'-the-Wisps. He was stumbling through the stinking mud, with creeping horrors plucking at his coat.

Summoning the last of her strength, the Moon shook off her hood. Light streamed from her silver hair, lighting up the swamp as if it were day. The bogles ran screeching for cover. Now the boy could see the path clearly, and headed for home.

The Moon was exhausted. She bowed her head and the hood slipped forward again, covering her hair. Now the bogles could see her clearly.

They came creeping out of their lairs, cackling with glee. They dragged
the Moon into their deepest, darkest bog-hole, blocked the entrance with
a heavy boulder, and slimed their way back to their hovels.

Days turned to weeks, and weeks to months. As dreary night followed
dreary night, the townsfolk began to wonder why the Moon had abandoned
them. No one dared to go into the dark swamp. As the bogles grew bolder,
they began to venture into the town. At night the townsfolk kept their doors
locked and their lanterns burning bright, for they knew that if their fires
went out, the bogles would come in.

One evening, the desperate townsfolk gathered in the tavern. Why had the
Moon abandoned them? Was the Earth about to fall from the heavens? Was
it a witch's curse? Then a young boy called Thomas shouted above the noise.

"I know where the Moon is!" he said.

Everyone listened as Thomas told them about the night he had been lost
in the swamp, and how he had been saved by a mysterious light.

"I think it was the Moon who saved me," said Thomas. "Perhaps she is a
prisoner of the bogles."

They decided to ask the advice of the wise old woman who lived at the
mill. When she heard Thomas' story, the old woman scratched her hairy
chin. She consulted a dusty book and looked into her crystal ball.

"What do you see?" asked Thomas.

"Darkness," she replied.

The old woman looked deeper into her crystal ball. "Now, this is what
you must do…"

Later that night, Thomas led a line of men across the swamp. Each
man was holding on tightly to the shoulder of the man in front. They could
see nothing, but they sensed the evil lying in wait and their hearts were icy
with fear. At last they came across a great boulder, lying half-submerged
in a gloomy pool. The men threw open their coats to reveal blazing
lanterns hidden beneath, and held them high in the darkness. Howling,
the bogles fled from the light.

The men worked quickly to move the boulder and finally rolled it away. As the muddy water cleared, a strange and haunting face appeared. Its beauty touched every heart. Luckily Thomas kept his wits about him. He plunged into the freezing water. He hacked through the tangled reeds and fought his way to where the Moon lay. Then he cut the ties that bound her.

There was a blinding flash and, like a comet, the Moon soared back into the heavens. She lit a bright path home for her rescuers, and drove the bogles down into the darkest depths of their slimy mire. And from that day to this, the Moon has remained in the sky.

So if you have to travel through Swampland at night, make sure the Moon is shining brightly – lighting up the shadows where the dark things wait.

The Star's Tears

Retold by Thomas H. Slone (Abridged)

Many mornings we see small drops of water on leaves, on stones, and on grass. The ancestors say this dew has a story. The ancestors' story goes as follows: long ago, before we existed, Star hung in the sky and spoke with Sand. The two had a contest.

Sand said to Star, "You and I must count how many of us there are. Who has more, sand or stars? Who will win?"

So Star and Sand began to count.

Sand counted how many stars there were in the sky. Then Star spoke, "Ok, you counted how many of me there are. Now I shall begin to count how many of you there are."

Sand lay down and fell deep asleep. Star counted and counted the grains of sand. But Sand was too numerous for Star to count. Star was able to count the grains of sand on the surface, but could not count the grains of sand below the surface. Sand won the contest, and Star was ashamed. Star was truly embarrassed. Tears welled up from Star's eyes and fell.

So in the morning we often see Star's tears on grass, on stones, and on tree leaves.

Being Free

By Christine Gustave

Like a seed
Carried by the wind
I dance away
From the world
To be free

Like a stream
And the sea
I integrate
With me and set
My mind free

Like the sun
I intend to be
Standing above
The world
Being free

Like a star
In the sky
One day
I will shine
Incessantly
Because there's freedom
Somewhere for me

WHY A RAINBOW FOLLOWS RAIN

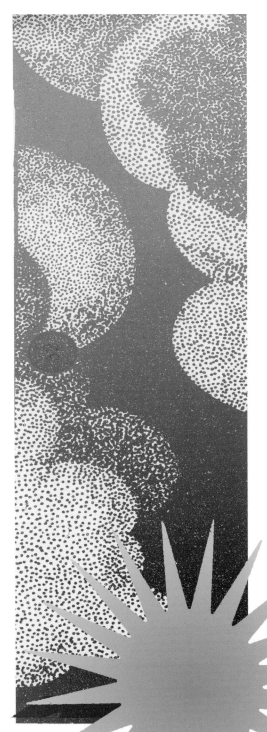

The Rainmaker

By Taia Teuai (An Extract)

f there is a long drought then I will make the rain fall.

First, I go to the bush to gather coconut leaves and flowers to weave myself a garland.

Later, towards sunset, I put oil over my body and, wearing a clean dress and with a garland on my head, go down to the beach to meet a team of 'rain makers'. These are little clouds sailing towards the setting sun.

I look at them and dance, and sing a song such as this one:

> *Little clouds, little clouds!*
> *Bring rain to me,*
> *To moisten my body.*

In three days time there will be heavy rain.

The Mist

By Mpho Mamashela

Slowly it comes creeping over the
mountains and tree tops,
like a small boy to a sleeping
grasshopper.

Not a leaf shakes nor twig cracks,
as it weaves its way through the
surrounding forests.

Like a lazy cat on a sleeping lap,
it settles on the sleeping hill,
to leave in the later hours, quietly
as it came,
unveiling the new day.

Rain and Fire

Retold by Linda Rode

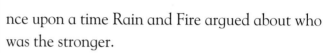

Once upon a time Rain and Fire argued about who was the stronger.

"Oh," boasted Rain in her silvery, watery voice, "I can make so much water fall upon the earth that the rivers are flooded and the houses are washed away completely."

"Humph," Fire answered in a smoky, husky voice, "so what? I can burn down woods and trees and houses so that nothing but black ashes remain."

Rain said: "You're not as strong as you think. I can quench your flames in an instant. They have no power against water."

Fire said: "Pooh, I'll soon dry your little streams with my heat."

"Let's see then," said Rain, and she gathered all the heaviest clouds together. Before long the first big drops began to fall. Fire took a seat on a dry camel-thorn log in the long grass and soon the first little flames were licking at the wood.

Then Wind came past. He looked at Fire and he looked at Rain and he said: "I'll help both of you. I'll whip the raindrops from the clouds and I'll chase along the flames. Then you can decide once and for all which one of you is stronger."

Rain made the water stream across the veld, but Fire quickly licked up all the water and dried out the veld.

A wise old tortoise that had floated to the top of an anthill said: "In water you can swim and survive, but against fire you can do nothing. Fire burns you to death."

Rain bowed her head and said: "Yes, that is true." And she went to hide high up in the clouds.

"Well, that's how it is then," said Wind and blew himself far away from Fire.

"I told you I am stronger," Fire cackled, but took care to call back his flames before they scorched the wise old tortoise.

Bringing the Rain to Kapiti Plain

By Verna Aardema (An Extract)

This is the cloud,
   all heavy with rain,
That shadowed the ground
   on Kapiti Plain.
This was the shot
   that pierced the cloud
And loosed the rain
   with thunder LOUD!
A shot from the bow,
   so long and strong,
And strung with a string,
   a leather thong;
A bow for the arrow
   Ki-pat put together,
With a slender stick
   and an eagle feather;
From the eagle who happened
   to drop a feather,
A feather that helped
   to change the weather.
It fell near Ki-pat,
   who watched his herd
As he stood on one leg,
   like the big stork bird;

Ki-pat, whose cows
    were so hungry and dry,
They mooed for the rain
    to fall from the sky;
To green-up the grass,
    all brown and dead,
That needed the rain
    from the cloud overhead –
The big, black cloud,
    all heavy with rain,
That shadowed the ground
    on Kapiti Plain.

The Storm

By Ashok B. Raha

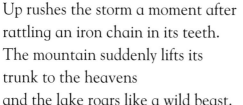

Without warning a snake of black
cloud rises in the sky.
It hisses as it runs and spreads its hood.
The moon goes out, the mountain is dark.
Far away is heard the shout of the demon.

Up rushes the storm a moment after
rattling an iron chain in its teeth.
The mountain suddenly lifts its
trunk to the heavens
and the lake roars like a wild beast.

The Thunder Spirit's Bride

Retold by Kathleen Arnott (Abridged)

Along time ago there lived a woman whose husband went off to fight with the other warriors in his tribe, leaving her at home alone, in a little hut, far away from other folk.

One morning when she awoke she felt too tired and ill to get up. She began to shiver with cold, and knowing that only a fire could make her feel better, she cried out loud: "Oh! What shall I do? If only I had someone to bring me firewood and light a fire, I should not care who it was! I would welcome even the Thunder Spirit himself, if he came."

The woman lay on her bed and looked out at the blue sky which showed through the cracks of her little wooden door. Presently she noticed that the sky was turning grey, and then the wind began to blow, first softly, then more and more fiercely.

"How strange!" she said to herself. "This is not the time of year for rain."

Suddenly there was a vivid flash of lightning and a great peal of thunder. The woman covered her eyes and screamed, and when she opened them again she saw a strange-looking man standing before her. His skin was as dark as the clouds but his eyes shone like the lightning, while his voice was deep and thunderous.

"You called me" he said, "and I have come to help you."

The woman was speechless with surprise. Before she could get her breath, he had hurried out of the hut, in the direction of the forest, and soon she heard the sound of his axe. In a short while he was back again, carrying a great pile of wood. Without a word, the Thunder Spirit stretched out his hand towards the twigs and spurts of fire, like lightning, shot from his fingers, turning the wood into a blazing fire.

Now the woman was terrified and hid her face under the blanket, but the Thunder Spirit said, in his booming voice: "Now! What will you give me for helping you? I have given you a fire to warm yourself and cook your food, and now you must give something to me in return."

The woman tried to speak, but her teeth were chattering so much with fear that she could not utter a sound.

"I will tell you what I want," shouted the Thunder Spirit. "Very soon you are to have a child. If your baby is a girl, will you give her to me for a wife?"

The poor woman was so anxious to get rid of the Thunder Spirit that she took a deep breath and whispered: "Yes!"

"Very well, then," replied the Thunder Spirit, and he immediately vanished in a flash of lightning.

For several days the fire burned and the woman gradually nursed herself back to health, so that when her husband returned she was waiting for him.

Some time afterwards, a baby girl was born to them, and they called her Miseke. The husband was delighted, but the woman wept and wailed and refused to be comforted.

"I cannot understand you," said her husband. "Here we have a lovely baby daughter, and yet you are sad. Why is this?"

At last the woman decided that she must tell her husband what had happened while he was away. Then he understood her fears, but he did not believe that any harm would come to his daughter.

"It will be many years yet before she is old enough to get married," he said. "By that time the Thunder Spirit will have forgotten all about her."

So the child grew from a baby to a little girl, and soon she was old enough to run about and help her mother in the fields. Little Miseke played with the other children in the village, swimming in the river and making tiny mud houses.

But one day her friends came running to her mother, shouting excitedly,

"Every time Miseke laughs, beads and bracelets drop from her mouth. Come and see!"

Miseke's mother ran down to the river, and there stood Miseke surrounded by beads and brass bangles, copper anklets and necklaces.

"Where do these things come from?" asked Miseke. "They are like the gifts a man gives to his bride, but I am not a bride."

Then her mother realised that the Thunder Spirit had not forgotten that Miseke had been promised to him. Seizing Miseke by the arm, she said: "Come home quickly. You must not play by the river any more."

Miseke and her companions could not understand why her mother was so worried, and when she kept Miseke shut up at home in the hut, and never allowed her to go out and play, the girls were even more puzzled.

Now one day, when Miseke was about fifteen years old, her parents had to go to their farm to harvest their yams, and so they left her locked up in the hut as usual. When the other girls in the village saw Miseke's parents go, they ran to the door of Miseke's hut and said: "Come with us, Miseke. We are going to the river."

Miseke was delighted at the chance to escape. Down to the river they went, and when they had splashed and swum about in the cool water, they came out again and began to dig up the white clay used for making their water-jars and cooking-pots. Miseke was helping her friends when one of them cried, "Look at the sky! It is growing so black, I think there will be a storm."

"But this is not the time of year for rain," said another. "How strange! I can hear thunder."

Suddenly, out of the clouds, in a flash of lightning, the Thunder Spirit appeared. He stood before the girls and said in his deep voice: "Which of you is Miseke?"

The girls were all too terrified to answer, and covering their eyes with their arms, they crowded together for safety.

The Thunder Spirit asked again: 'Which one of you is Miseke? I have come to take her back with me."

At this, one of the girls found her voice, for she was determined that the Thunder Spirit should not take her away. "I am not Miseke," she cried. "When she laughs, beads and bangles drop from her lips."

"Let me see you laugh, then," said the Thunder Spirit, and when the girl laughed and nothing happened, he stood aside and let her pass and she ran swiftly back to her home.

One by one the girls were made to laugh, until only Miseke was left.

"Let me see you laugh," said the Thunder Spirit, and when beads and bangles fell to the ground, he said quite kindly, but very loudly: "Then you are my promised bride, and I shall take you back to my home in the sky."

Seizing Miseke round the waist, he flew upwards in a flash of lightning, and nobody ever saw her again.

But that is not the end of the story. Miseke was very happy up in the sky. Her husband provided her with everything she could possibly wish for, and later on she had three children. Their father taught them how to travel through the air on flashes of lightning, and they had a much more exciting life than the children of the earth, who could only walk and run. Miseke had no desire to fly about with the rest of her family, but she did as she wished, and had a much happier time than if she had lived on in the village of her girlhood.

111

Mookari

By Dan Davis

I think it's going to rain today, the sun isn't so bright.
The clouds are slowly covering the blue, closing it from sight.

He coming now, I think I hear some thunder, smell rain in the air.
Just saw a flash of lightning, stretching out over there.

"BANG," the clap of thunder goes, it can give a little fright.
Watching this lightning can be dangerous, but oh what a sight!

He coming now, see I told you he'll be back to see us all soon.
The old fella, always brings the lightning, and noisy thunder too.

He coming now, for how long I can't really say.
But he here for a little while, so don't go outside and play.

He here now, look how he lights up the sky.
That old fella Mookari, he don't wanna say goodbye.

Look how he makes the thunder roar so very loud.
He makes the lightning show it's brightness, he feeling really proud.

Mookari old man, you're the same every year.
I like it when you visit us, but don't get too near.

Mookari old man, the name for real big rain.
Looks like the old man is going now but he'll be back again.

He going now, the rain is slowing down.
He'll go and water somewhere else, cool off some other town.

There he goes, the sky is turning blue, the sun is coming out.
But watch out for that old man, he'll come back to us no doubt.

Invocation to the Rainbow

Traditional Chant

Rainbow, O Rainbow,
You who shine away up there, so high,
Above the forest that is so vast,
Among the black clouds,
Dividing the dark sky.

You have overturned,
You have wrestled down
The thunder that roared,
Roared so loud, in rage!
Was it angry against us?

Among the black clouds,
Dividing the dark sky,
As a knife cuts through an over-ripe fruit,
Rainbow, Rainbow!

And it fled,
The thunder killer of men,
Like the antelope from the panther,
Rainbow, Rainbow!

Strong bow of the Hunter above,
The Hunter who hunts down the herd of clouds
Like a herd of elephants in terror,
Rainbow, speak our thanks to him
Say to him: 'Be not angry!'
Say to him: 'Be not wrathful!'
Say to him: 'Kill us not!'
For we are greatly afraid,
Rainbow, tell him so!

GHOSTS, GIANTS
AND
MERMAIDS
OF THE
DEEP

Wind and River Romance

By John Agard

Wind forever playing loverboy
bringing he breeze joy
to everything he touch
but Wind you can't trust

Forever playing fresh
with big woman like me
He forget I name River –
passing he hand over me face
tickling me bellyskin
talking to me in whisper

Promising to bring down
the moon and the stars
and lay them in me lap
even when hot sun shining
but sweet whispering don't catch me

I know Wind too good
I does just flow along to faithful Sea
and let Wind sweet words pass by
like cool breeze

When I was a Child...

By M. NourbeSe Philip *(An Extract)*

Lamplight, fireflight, soft lies
and rounded eyes a listening table,
floating fiery tales of socouyants
lacing the edge of night with
lamplight, softlight and fireflies,
worms of delight tickle
curls of toes rooted in safety large laps
secure from little dwens with feet turned
backwards and lajablesse
the cloven footed siren
far from the soft light, lamplight and firelight

Tebwere, Tebarere, and Tetintiri

Retold by Bo Flood et al. (Abridged)

Once, on an island in Kiribati, three boys lived with their mother. The children were not very obedient. They always ran away from their mother and did naughty things.

They lived on the north end of their island and were allowed to play in the lagoon all day. There was only one rule: they were NEVER to go to the south end of the island, for a giant lived there and would eat them.

Of course, the boys could not wait to go to the south end of the island. One day, when their mother was taking a nap, they quietly ran out of their hut and down the path leading south. They did not believe the giant was real. Besides, they knew magic and could take care of themselves.

When they got to the south end of the island, they found a large pool of clear water that was full of fish. Just across the pool stood a hut. There was no one around. The boys were hot from their walk. The pool looked so good that before you could say, "Don't do that," they did. They jumped right into the pool and began to splash and play. By the time they were done, the clear water was all muddy.

Suddenly a large voice called out, "Who is playing in the giant's pool?" Then a huge old woman came out of the hut. "I see you naughty children! You are lucky that my husband is taking a nap! Now you better go away before you get into trouble."

The boys were not only naughty, but they were also rude. They teased the old woman and called her names. Now the woman was angry. "I will tell the giant about you and you will be in big trouble. Now tell me your names!"

"We are Tebwere, Tebarere, and Tetintiri," they answered. Then the children giggled and the youngest chanted a magic spell:

Old lady, old lady, this spell will tie your tongue
And you will never tell by whom this deed was done.

When the giant woke from his nap, he asked "Who dirtied my pool?"

"Three naughty boys," his wife replied.

"Well, tell me their names," demanded the giant. But his wife could only stammer. No matter how hard she tried she could not say the names of the boys.

The next day, the boys returned to the pool. This time they went fishing. They caught every one of the giant's special fish.

Once again the great voice boomed, "Who is there fishing in the giant's pool?" Once again the children cast their spell on the poor woman's tongue.

That night the giant went to his pool to catch some fish. The pool was empty. All the fish were gone. "Who has been catching my fish?" he demanded. His wife could only stammer.

The giant and his wife decided it was time to punish these boys. They began to follow the tracks the careless children had left in the sand. The tracks led straight to their little hut in the north!

Soon the giant and his wife came near the hut where the children lived. "I will catch you now!" the giant roared. He began to walk up to the hut. However, although the giant started right toward the hut, he suddenly found himself on a beach far to the east. He had missed the hut entirely! "How did I get here?" he wondered. "I know the hut is in the north. I will be more careful." This time the giant found himself far to the west. No matter how hard he tried, his feet seemed to have a mind of their own and led him to every place except to the hut.

This giant was not so stupid as the children thought. "Hmmmm," he thought. "My feet will not walk in a straight line. So maybe I will just crawl on my hands and knees. This way I will go right underneath their magic."

That is just what he did, right up to the hut. Then he ate the hut and everyone in it. And this is the end of my story.

The Enchanted Rock

By Clarita Richards

In the deep blue Pacific stands a rock as black as night,
And there upon it sits a lonely mermaid
Her scaly body shining in the light.
From daybreak until twilight she sits and combs her hair,
Twining them in curls around her body fair.

She looks not neither left nor right
Nor even up nor down;
But she stares straight before her
And her forehead wears a frown.

Once some shipwrecked mariners
Were thrown upon her realm,
They had no rafts to bear them home,
Their ship she had no helm.

Frightened yet desperate, they clambered up its side,
As a half-smashed ship will sail, before the dangerous tide
And once upon the rock, they knew their hour had come
For there was no earthly way for a ship to bear them home.

Early the next morning a ship from their homeland came,
With a flag above her helm and around her prow her name;
But when they espied the rock they saw the mermaid there,
But of the wretched seamen there was no sign, nowhere.

The Warrior Women of Lumalao

Adapted from a retelling by Bo Flood et al.

nce, in the time before, ghosts, called *gosile*, flew about the sky looking for humans to eat. When they flew, the wind rushed through their long hair, making an eerie noise – "*Whooeeeeiii.*" Those who heard this sound knew that *gosile* were nearby.

On this one day, two young women were walking near their village. They strolled together, picking flowers and talking about their husbands and families.

Suddenly, disaster struck. Two *gosile* were flying overhead. When the first looked down, he saw the two women on the road far below. "Look at that," he said to his companion. "I think I see our dinner walking down that road!"

With that, the two *gosile* flew down and captured the women. Now *gosile* are very strong, and it did no good for the women to resist. They cried and screamed, but the *gosile* carried them off.

The *gosile* flew to their home on Saraainonganonga, far out in the ocean. There they set their captives down while they sharpened their stone axes.

"Please don't eat us!" the women cried. And the two *gosile*, who weren't all that hungry, decided not to eat them just yet. But they would not let the women return to their homes.

Meanwhile, on the mainland, the women's husbands were organising a rescue party. A huge reward was offered for the safe return of the women and the killing of the evil *gosile*. Young betel nut trees, coconuts, porpoise teeth, pigs with huge tusks, and, most valuable, one hundred strings of shell money, would be given to the warrior who killed the monsters.

Many tried, and failed, to claim this reward. A rescue party of one hundred canoes returned empty-handed. Many of the crew had been carried off by the *gosile*. The villagers gave up hope.

"What can we do?" they asked. "The *gosile* are stronger than any man."

On Saraainonganonga, the two women cried out: "Is there no man to save us from these monsters?"

There wasn't.

But there was a woman.

Word of the plight of the women, and of the huge reward offered for their rescue, spread far and wide. One day it reached the island of Lumalao. There lived a fierce group of warrior women and their leader, Riina.

"Is this true?" wondered Riina. "Is this large reward offered just for killing two *gosile*?"

Riina travelled to the island of the husbands and offered to kill the *gosile*. The villagers thought she was boasting. This made Riina very angry. She stamped her feet and announced, "These are just *gosile*. And male *gosile* at that!"

With that, Riina paddled back to Lumalao and gathered her large fighting group of women. Together they set out looking for the *gosile*.

The band paddled from island to island. Finally they neared the island of Saraainonganonga.

"*Whooeeeiii.*" The eerie sound floated over the waves.

"This is the place," announced Riina. "Everyone hide." Riina alone stood up in the canoe. When the *gosile* saw a canoe approaching with only a single woman, they were not concerned. One of the *gosile*, Otabulau, flew down at her carrying his sharp stone axe. He intended to kill Riina and eat her for his supper!

Instead, Riina grabbed Otabulau's hair and threw him into the canoe. There all the other women tied him to the bottom of the boat.

"Where do you get your power?" she asked. The frightened *gosile* replied, "From betel, lime, and my red stone axe." As he spoke these words, these very objects fell from his body into the bottom of the canoe.

Riina carefully and slowly stepped right over these sacred objects. It was, of course, taboo for any woman to step over sacred objects. When she did so, her female essence instantly took away all the power of Otabulau's axe, betel, and lime.

The canoe landed. The women took the bound Otabulau and climbed to the *gosile's* cave. They found Nuitarara, the second *gosile*, nearby. Riina turned on the *gosile* and drew out her special weapon. A boomerang! With this weapon she struck the startled *gosile* and killed them both in an instant. Then she took the two captive women and they began the long trip back to their island.

It took six days of paddling to get back to the village. The husbands and village were so happy to get their wives back and be rid of the *gosile* that they prepared a huge feast.

Thus these warrior women did what no man had been able to do. Many other tales are told of Riina and her band, but they must be kept for another time.

Kyrenia

By Nora Nadjarian

Imagine it, says my mother. Kyrenia.
Standing at the edge of ripples,
an orange sun on my hair,
zest on my skin.

Boats dancing in water, floating
like smiles at a wedding, on white light.
Mermaid voices gliding in and out
of nets, shimmers of songs.

Like my youth, she says, out of reach.
At times, she weeps; till sun meets moon,
till mermaids scream and boats turn
to rocks about to sink.

Rampunch and the Sea Devil

Adapted from a retelling by Nadrien McIntyre

here was a time, very long ago, when fishermen used to deal with the sea-devil. The sea-devil owned everything in the sea. If you were a fisherman and wanted to get rich quick, all you had to do was to make a deal with the sea-devil to give you a good catch each time, and what you gave in return was a male human soul.

In the little fishing village of Grand Roy, there was a fisherman named Jarbeau. He was the richest man in Grand Roy and he had the biggest belly.

One day a stranger came to live in Grand Roy. His name was Rampunch Rattal and he was a very covetous fisherman. When he saw Jarbeau's way of life he was interested. He had heard of men who dealt with the sea-devil and had long wanted to do the same; but he dared not ask back home, for those people were very religious. Now this was his big chance.

But Jarbeau was wise and when Rampunch approached him he turned him down stating that he knew of no such thing. But Rampunch was a very persistent man and he kept at Jarbeau until he told him all that he was supposed to do.

There was a big rock jutting out into the sea from the beach; he was to go twelve miles out from there, on the twelfth of any month, and he was to be there at twelve o'clock, midnight. He would then have to wait in his boat and the sea-devil would come to him.

Rampunch was glad it was all so very easy. He looked at the almanac. By gosh! Today was the twelfth. He would go this very night. All day Rampunch planned what he would say to the sea-devil when he saw him.

He thought to himself, "When I, Rampunch, meet the sea-devil ah go tell him me name and wey ah from. Ah have a boat, an' a wife. Anything you wants me to do, ah go do".

So at five minutes to twelve Rampunch was on the spot. The night was dark and cold and the water was calm. He had put on a very heavy jacket to keep out the cold as he waited alone.

At twelve o'clock on the dot, things began to happen. The calm sea started to roll, the waves began to rise and fall steadily. All around him he heard shouts. He had not bargained for this stormy weather and got scared. Lord help him.

He was so far out to sea that he had lost the true image of Grand Roy. At a distance he saw a few lights way up north and that was all. The boat started to heave and he was tossed from side to side. The water showed jet black in the dark; like a giant killer. All of a sudden he saw a huge shape approaching, dark as the night itself. The boat became very hot. To feel heat, of all things, on a cold night like this was something else. Lord! What was that huge black thing?

He heard a voice saying, "What do you want? Why did you call me?"

"Oh Mercy, who dat you be, ah din call you. Have pity on meh, doh kill meh".

"I am the sea-devil, what do you want?"

By this time the huge form was covering the small boat. Rampunch was scared to death. The boat was as hot as the hottest furnace in hell and he could not see a thing. The boat still rocked dangerously, pitching him from side to side. Lord what was he going to do! He had lost his oars and he couldn't swim. What was he going to do?

Maybe if he said Jarbeau sent him things might be easier as Jarbeau dealt with this huge creature. So he stuttered that Jarbeau had sent him. Well this was all the sea-devil wanted to hear, for Jarbeau owed him a soul that night.

Before Rampunch knew what was happening he was hurled headlong into the black choppy waters never to be seen again.

WATER GODS
AND
ICE KINGS

The Water God's Challenge

Retold by Vic Parker (Abridged)

lokun was the great god of water. He lived deep down in the sea in a magical palace and he owned a mighty river that filled all the oceans of the world.

The men and women of Nigeria loved Olokun and worshipped him as their favourite god. They built him amazing temples and decorated them with expensive materials and delicately carved figures. People had statues of Olokun in their houses and prayed to the mighty god every day.

All this worshipping made Olokun feel very important. So important, in fact, that he became quite bigheaded.

I shouldn't just be the god of water, Olokun began to think. *I should really be the chief god!*

The thought niggled away at Olokun until one day he exploded at his servant, "What can the chief god do for humans that I can't?"

"Um… um… I don't know!" the startled servant spluttered.

"Exactly!" roared the water god. "That's why I'm sending you to the chief god with a message. Tell him that I challenge him for his title of chief god!"

The servant gulped.

"Yes, my lord," he squeaked nervously. He dashed away to the chief god's palace, panicking all the way. Surely the chief god would be furious at such a bold message!

When the servant was shown into the chief god's magnificent chamber, his teeth were chattering and his knees knocking with fear. He bowed low before the chief god's enormous throne.

"Y-y-your m-m-majesty…" the servant stuttered. "Y-y-your r-r-royal h-h-highness…"

"Enough!" the chief god commanded. "I can read the thoughts of all creatures and I know why you have come"

The servant shut his eyes tightly and waited to be sent to the dungeons.

"Tell your master that I accept his challenge."

The stunned servant couldn't believe his ears.

"Of course, I am far too busy to meet Olokun myself," the chief god continued, with a secret smile. "I will send a messenger instead."

The servant scurried backwards out of the room, bowing all the way, and ran to Olokun with the news.

At first, the water god wasn't pleased at all.

"A messenger?" Olokun thundered. "I challenge the chief god and he sends a *messenger*?"

The servant thought quickly. "Perhaps the chief god is afraid to face you himself, my lord," he suggested.

"You must be right!" Olokun crowed. "I'll soon show this nobody of a messenger exactly what he is up against."

Olokun barked orders and hundreds of servants sprang into action, dashing here, there and everywhere. By the time a fanfare announced the arrival of the chief god's messenger, Olokun's underwater palace sparkled and glittered. Coral tables were laid with delicious food. Beautiful music rippled through every room and the floors shone with a million colourful shells.

Finally, the water god himself strode into his throne room. He was dressed splendidly in amazing robes that swirled and billowed like the waves of the ocean.

The moment Olokun caught sight of the messenger, he stopped dead in his tracks. The messenger was wearing the same clothes as he was!

"Will you excuse me for a minute?" Olokun muttered. "I really must change out of these old rags."

The water god hurried back to his dressing room, his face red with embarrassment.

It wasn't long before Olokun was back. This time, he was wearing robes that clung around him and shimmered like sea mist. Yet Olokun had no sooner laid eyes on the messenger than he turned and headed out again.

"Do forgive me!" he shouted over his shoulder. "I have spotted a speck of dirt on my robes. Allow me to change. Somehow, the messenger's clothes again matched Olokun's outfit!

When Olokun entered the throne room for the third time, everyone gasped. The water god was dressed in the very best clothes he owned. They were so rich and fine he had never even worn them before. Olokun had been saving them for when he became the new chief god. As he walked, the robes rippled and changed from the colours of sunrise, to sunset, to starry midnight. They rustled and swished with the secret songs of ancient sea creatures. No one had ever seen anything so beautiful.

Imagine Olokun's horror when he saw that the messenger had changed his clothes, too. Once again they were both wearing exactly the same robes!

Olokun realised he was beaten. He bowed his head in shame.

"Go back to the chief god," he whispered. "Give him my respects and tell him I have learned my lesson. I cannot compete with the chief god's messenger, let alone the chief god himself."

The water god never found out that the chief god's messenger was really a chameleon – an animal that changes its colours to match its surroundings. Olokun had been tricked by nature itself.

Mawu of the Waters

By Abena P. A. Busia

I am Mawu of the Waters.
With mountains as my footstool
And stars in my curls
I reach down to reap the waters with my fingers
And look! I cup lakes in my palms.
I fling oceans around me like a shawl
And am transformed
Into a waterfall.
Springs flow through me
And spill rivers at my feet
As fresh streams surge
To make seas.

The River Fairy

Adapted from a retelling by Rosetta Baskerville

ne day, a very long time ago, a little orphaned girl was sitting, hungry and sad, beside the river Nile. She had a very, very, *very* long name, which means 'Glory'. As Glory stared into the rushing river, she saw the tail of a great fish as it turned in the water. The girl was a little frightened, for she had never seen such a huge fish in the river before. To her surprise, as it came nearer, she saw that it had a woman's head and that half of its body was that of a woman. The fish-woman spoke to her:

"Do not be afraid, little girl; I have seen you here very often, and I want to be your friend. Tell me your sorrow."

"I am all alone, and I cannot live all by myself," said Glory. "I don't know what to do." And she began to cry.

The fish-woman came nearer and pulled herself up on a rock, and Glory stopped crying to look at the beautiful tail covered with golden-brown scales which flashed in the sunlight as the drops of water ran from it.

"What a beautiful tail you have!" she said.

"I am the Fairy of the river Nile," said the fish-woman, "and we all have beautiful tails in my country."

"Where is your country?" asked Glory.

"You see the Great Lake which stretches away above the Ripon Falls? Under those blue waters, far, far down lies a beautiful country. It is not like the country you know, but has fields of soft green seaweed, forests of great sea-palms, sea-flowers of every colour and shade. In the middle of this country is the Lake City where the King of the Fish-people lives, a wonderful city of caves cut in the rocks. There are long streets full of blue water, and

138

the caves are the homes of the Fish-people. There is one cave larger and more beautiful than the others, and that is the King's palace. He has given us each a job to do. Mine is to watch the entrance of the river Nile. All day I live in my cave under the Falls, and at sunset I swim by a passage through the rock into the Great Lake above, and go to give my day's report to the King. There are other fairies who guard the entrance of rivers which flow into the Great Lake, but mine is the only river which flows out of it. My river dashes over the Falls and hurries away to the Rapids, and on and on, through deserts and plains till it reaches another Great Sea."

"I would love to see your cave and your Lake City," said Glory. "How can I become a fish-maiden?"

"It needs a great deal of courage for a mortal to join us. I would have to cut off your feet, and from them a tail would grow."

Glory looked down at her little brown feet and dug her toes in and out of the soft sand, and said: "I don't want my feet cut off."

The fish-woman tossed her head and slipped off her rock into the foaming water. Within a few seconds she had disappeared under the Falls.

That night Glory watched the big red sun drop down behind the hills, and quickly the darkness fell round her. She crept into her cold, empty hut, and shut the reed door, and tried to get warm under the barkcloths; but the night was damp and foggy, and she shivered all alone. She heard the owls hooting to each other outside, and the bats squealing as they hung on to the porch of the hut for a minute or two on their way to hunt. Glory passed a long, sleepless night.

When dawn flashed streaks of light across the sky, she hurried down to the river, and there sat the fish-woman on the same rock, her golden-brown tail catching the rays of the rising sun.

"O River Fairy," she cried. "I have changed my mind! I want to come and live in the Great Lake with you!" The fish-woman smiled and bound Glory's legs together with broad bands of seaweed. Then she picked up a large, sharp shell. Glory looked at her little brown feet one last time and then

UGANDA

whoosh the River Fairy's shell came slicing down. All at once a little tail appeared where Glory's feet had been a moment before.

Quickly the fish-woman slipped into the water and carried Glory to her cave under the Falls. She laid her on a lovely soft bed of seaweed. There Glory slept for a whole week and every day her tail grew more beautiful, and when she woke it looked like mother o' pearl.

Many years later, on a day when the sun had set and fires had been lit in the fishermen's huts near the river Nile, and the people had eaten their evening meal and gathered round the fire to tell stories, an old fisherman spoke with wonder of a giant fish he had seen near the Falls, with the head and shoulders of a woman. The other fishermen laughed at the old man's tale, and shook their heads in disbelief.

But you and I know better, for the old fisherman had seen Glory, the Fish-maiden, who is now the River Fairy and guards the Ripon Falls. Here the Great Lake sends its blue waters over the rocks, and they hurry away foaming towards the Rapids, and on and on over the deserts and plains carrying greetings from the Great Lake to the Great Sea which lies far away to the North.

The Ice King

By A. B. Demille

Where the world is grey and lone
Sits the Ice King on his throne –

Passionless, austere, afar,
Underneath the Polar Star.

Over all his splendid plains
An eternal stillness reigns.

Silent creatures of the North,
White and strange and fierce, steal forth:

Soft-foot beasts from frozen lair,
Noiseless birds that wing the air,

Souls of seamen dead, who lie
Stark beneath the pale north sky;

Shapes to living eye unknown,
Wild and shy, come round the throne

Where the Ice King sits in view
To receive their homage due.

But the Ice King's quiet eyes,
Calm, implacable, and wise,

Gaze beyond the silent throng,
With a steadfast look and long,

Down to where the summer streams
Murmur in their golden dreams;

Where the sky is rich and deep,
Where warm stars bring down warm sleep,

Where the days are, every one,
Clad with warmth and crowned with sun.

And the longing gods may feel
Stirs within his heart of steel,

And he yearns far forth to go
From his land of ice and snow.

But forever, grey and lone,
Sits the Ice King on his throne –

Passionless, austere, afar,
Underneath the Polar Star.

The Marriage of the Rain Goddess

Retold by Margaret Olivia Wolfson (Abridged)

he earth people loved the rain goddess. When they heard the BOOM! BOOM! of her thunder-drum they knew the rains would come.

Still, the rain goddess was lonely. She longed for a companion. She wanted a mate to share the joy she felt when, peeking through the clouds, she observed sea snails floating on crystal bubbles, eland and antelope drinking from pools, and crickets and frogs croaking and singing on moon-gold nights.

In search of a partner, the rain goddess journeyed through the heavens. But though the gods were handsome, fearless and strong, they stirred no love in her heart. They were too busy with their spears and shields.

And so the rain goddess decided to seek her husband among the mortals. She changed herself into a shaft of sunlight and in glittering golden beams fell to the village below her hut. With radiant eyes, she peered through open doorways, watching the people as they ate and talked, cooked and slept, and polished their earthen floors until they gleamed like black pearls. But no man here moved her heart.

Finally, after many months of wandering, her eyes came to rest on a young cattle-herder named Thandiwe. Thandiwe was returning to the kraal, singing as he went. The beauty of his music told the goddess much about the depth of his heart. Still, he was a mortal. He must be tested. Smiling, the goddess returned to her rainbow hut, a gleaming curtain of rain falling from each footstep.

144

That night, Thandiwe had a dream. In his dream he saw a magical being, glistening in oil and golden bracelets, her face half-hidden by twisted leaves. She handed him a small square of coloured beads. Thandiwe knew the meaning of many of the colours. The white told him her love was pure; the brown that it was as rich as earth; and the blue that she would fly across endless skies to meet him.

The magical woman then said, "You are destined to marry Mbaba Mwana Waresa, the rain goddess. When you awake, begin building the iqati, the bridal home. When the hut is finished, stand before it. No matter what happens, wait there for your bride."

When Thandiwe awoke, he shook his head in disbelief. Resting in his hand was a love letter of coloured beads.

The next day, Thandiwe began building his bridal hut. When it was finished, he stood before it and waited.

As Thandiwe waited, the rain goddess prepared for her marriage. She shaved her head, and covered it with a ragged cloth. She removed her rainbow-coloured skirt and wrapped herself in a torn zebra skin. She smeared her beautiful brown skin with ashes. Then she summoned a young girl named Nomalanga to her rainbow hut.

The goddess dressed Nomalanga in the costume of the Zulu bride. She draped coils of coloured beads around the girl's neck and waist and covered her face with a veil of twisted leaves. She circled Nomalanga's wrists with gold and copper and adorned her with polished pebbles and shells. She rubbed her skin with oil until it glistened like sunlight on water. When she had finished, the goddess stepped back and smiled. Nomalanga was beautiful.

Meanwhile, Thandiwe continued to wait. "Look at the fool!" a villager shouted, "He thinks he is getting married, but no girl has been promised him. Thandiwe! You are crazier than the hyena who tries to catch the moon's reflection in its jaws!"

Suddenly, storm clouds gathered on the horizon and jagged streaks of lightning flashed across the sky.

"It's the Lightning Bird!" the villagers cried in terrified voices as they scurried for shelter. Thandiwe shuddered, fear clawing at his heart. But he remained in front of the bridal hut, steadfastly awaiting the magical woman seen in his dreams.

Then, as quickly as it had come, the storm passed and a rainbow slid down from the heavens.

When the rainbow touched the ground, two women stepped from the shimmering bow. Looking Thandiwe in the eye and pointing to Nomalanga, the rain goddess said, "This is the beautiful being you saw in your dream. This is your bride."

Thandiwe regarded the girl, shining like a vision. Then he looked at the woman who had spoken. She was dull and grey, her head covered in rags.

"This girl is not my bride," said Thandiwe. "You may be dressed in torn zebra skins and covered with ashes, but these things cannot conceal your splendour. In your eyes, I see the bright gleam of rivers, ponds, lakes and seas. In your eyes, I see the power of one who greens the earth and nourishes the crops. Such power far surpasses the charm of well-oiled skin and the jingling of bracelets and cowry shells. You are my bride. You are Mbaba Mwana Waresa, the rain goddess."

When the goddess heard these words, she knew she had chosen wisely. "Let the ceremonies begin," she said.

Soon the villagers were dancing and feasting, celebrating the marriage of Mbaba Mwana Waresa and Thandiwe. It was only when the sun dipped behind the hills and the stars sparkled – silver beads in the sky, that the festivities came to an end.

While everyone was sleeping, Mbaba Mwana Waresa and Thandiwe left the earth. Hand in hand, they journeyed to the rainbow hut, high up in the African heavens. And there they live to this very day and will always live, for Thandiwe had become a god, and like the souls of mortal men and women, gods and goddesses never die.

GLOSSARY

The following are terms, expressions, mythological creatures and characters from folklore that originate in languages and cultures other than English. They are explained below, by country, in the order they appear in the stories and poems.

SAMOA – *frangipani, sandlewood, mosooi, gardenia*: types of fragrant flowering plants found in Samoa.

MALAWI – *chambo*: a type of fish found in Lake Malawi, located between Malawi, Mozambique and Tanzania.

SWAZILAND – *Nkalimeva*: a fantastic creature, often imagined to have evil intentions. In Xhosa folklore it is more frequently referred to as 'Inkalimeva'. The Xhosa people are an ethnic group living primarily in south-eastern South Africa.

TANZANIA – *chungu; Kwa heri ya kuonana, wanangu*: Swahili word and phrase (translated within the text).

NEW ZEALAND – *Tangaroa*: the god of the sea in Maori mythology, son of Rangi (sky) and Papa (earth). The sea-god is said to have given birth to all sea creatures.

SEYCHELLES – *karang*: the Creole word for a type of fish found in the waters off the coast of the Seychelles.

BANGLADESH – *saree*: often spelt 'sari', a long piece of cloth worn as a dress by many women in Bangladesh.

UNITED KINGDOM – *Will-o'-the-wisps*: ignited marsh gas sometimes seen above marshes and swampland. These ghostly lights often appear in myths and legends as mischievous sprites leading travellers astray.

UNITED KINGDOM – *bogles*: an old-fashioned word for 'bogey' or 'hobgoblin', a frightening creature of folklore from Northumbria in the north of England and Scotland.

NAMIBIA – *veld*: the open plains of Southern Africa. Rain and Fire are mythological characters in the folklore of the Damara peoples of Namibia.

KENYA – *Kapiti Plain*: open plains stretching to the south of Nairobi, Kenya's capital city. The poem is based on a tale told by the Nandi peoples of Kenya.

RWANDA – *The Thunder Spirit*: named 'Nkuba' and worshipped in Rwanda as the god of lightning, thunder and fire.

AUSTRALIA – *Mookari*: the word used by the aboriginal Baradah Clan to mean 'storm'.

TRINIDAD AND TOBAGO – *socouyants*: often spelt 'soucouyant', a female spirit of folklore. This spirit, resembling a vampire, takes the form of an old woman during the day, and becomes a fireball at night, entering people's houses through keyholes to suck their blood.

TRINIDAD AND TOBAGO – *dwen*: often spelt 'douen', a spirit in Trinidad and Tobago folklore with feet turned backwards, said to represent the lost souls of children who have not been baptised or christened.

TRINIDAD AND TOBAGO – *lajablesse*: often known as 'la diablesse', a supernatural female devil with one human foot and one cloven hoof.

CYPRUS – *Kyrenia*: a town on the northern coast of Cyprus.

NIGERIA – *Olokun*: god of the ocean in the folklore of Nigeria and other parts of West Africa, known for his immense wisdom. Olokun can be male or female depending on the area of West Africa in which he/she is worshipped. In her more popular female incarnation, she is worshipped as the mother of all creation.

GHANA – *Mawu*: creator and moon goddess in the mythology of the Dahomey peoples (now known as the Fon peoples of Benin).

UGANDA – *Great Lake*: Africa's largest lake – Lake Victoria – located between Uganda, Kenya and Tanzania. The Ripon Falls is a waterfall at the northern end of the lake, often thought to be the source of the Nile.

SOUTH AFRICA – *kraal*: an enclosure for cattle within a village.

SOUTH AFRICA – *Mbaba Mwana Waresa*: Zulu goddess of rain, farming and the harvest. She is also the goddess of the rainbow, connecting the earth to the heavens, and men and women to the gods.

SOUTH AFRICA – *Zulu*: the largest ethnic group in South Africa, known for its beautiful beadwork. Messages are passed from one person to the next through the colour combinations chosen for the beadwork.

SOUTH AFRICA – *Lightning Bird*: known as 'Impundulu' in Zulu mythology, a human-sized black and white bird with evil intentions that shoots lightning from its talons.

The Commonwealth Education Trust

In 1837 a slight but strong-willed teenager ascended the British throne. Fifty years later Queen Victoria had established the monarchy and her own presence at the heart of the nation's identity. She was not merely Queen of the United Kingdom but Empress of India and titular head of the greatest empire the world had ever seen.

Edward, Prince of Wales, resolved that this fiftieth anniversary should be celebrated in a way which would unite all the peoples of the Empire. He decided upon the foundation of an Imperial Institute to undertake research, education and related activities which would promote the prosperity and development of that Empire. Supported by the Lord Mayor of London he set about raising the money, writing personally to friends and communities across the globe to promote the idea. A central organising committee was formed and local campaigns sprang up in towns and villages across the Empire. The Jubilee became a major Empire-wide public event with donations, however small, going to help fund the Institute and local civil facilities. Overwhelmingly the money came from individuals; the top-up from overseas publicly held funds was minor.

The Prince, as President of the campaign, remained closely involved in the project from its inception in late 1886 until his own accession to the throne 15 years later. The campaign raised £426,000 in cash and received a grant from the Royal Commission for the Exhibition of 1851 of six and three-quarter acres of land valued at £250,000. The culmination of this endeavour was the Imperial Institute building designed by Thomas Edward Collcutt and opened by Queen Victoria on 10 May 1893. The Queen, greatly affected by this manifestation of popular generosity and affection, became very attached to what she termed informally "my institute".

In the 125 years since the launch of the appeal the world has changed beyond recognition. The Empire has given way to a Commonwealth of 54 countries, a voluntary association of equal members united by a framework

150

of common values. The Institute is now the Commonwealth Education Trust – entrusted with the funds originating in the great public subscription. The great-great-granddaughter of Queen Victoria, Queen Elizabeth II, celebrates her sixtieth anniversary as Head of the Commonwealth in 2012.

A River of Stories travels over those 125 years – and articulates the fund's hopes for the future. The Trust sees its history as a river, bubbling into life, full of enthusiasm and ambition, and tumbling through some of the very rocky terrain of the 20th century. In the first decade of this century the flow virtually ceased, and its Trustees worked hard to keep the fund – and the river – alive. They have channelled the remaining resources into enhancing opportunities for the children of the Commonwealth to develop the skills to contribute to their communities' economic and social growth, notably by developing innovative learning materials and teaching methods based on careful research.

The anthology is intended to be read by children both for sheer pleasure and as a teaching aid at home and in schools. The theme of water is intensely relevant today when we are increasingly concerned about global warming, rising sea levels, species extinction, climate-related natural disasters and the need to feed a rising world population. The theme of water underlines the fragility of the earth, and the need for creative learning to stimulate the imagination when our every decision has the potential to change the lives of future generations.

In helping to equip children with the tools to enable them to make the choices which will benefit their communities the Trust is keeping alive the vision, ambition and enthusiasm which led to its creation.

We thank those of you who have purchased this book for your part in keeping the river flowing.

JUDITH C HANRATTY CVO OBE   THE RT HON THE LORD FELLOWES GCB GCVO QSO

JG (ALGY) CLUFF   HELEN ROBINSON OBE

TRUSTEES OF THE COMMONWEALTH EDUCATION TRUST

A Note from the Anthologist

In bringing together tales from around the world, I hope to have offered our readers glimpses into different cultures and their storytelling traditions. This collection does not attempt to represent any country as a whole, rather celebrate the unique imaginative heritage of many of the cultures encompassed by the Commonwealth. I have reproduced some tales word for word; others I have had to abridge or adapt slightly to make them accessible to an international child readership. I have juxtaposed well-loved tales with lesser-known myths, folktales and contemporary pieces and placed up-and-coming authors alongside established storytellers in the spirit of enlarging the space for new tales and new voices within the growing canon of Commonwealth children's literature.

Whilst a diminishing use of local languages is of serious issue throughout the Commonwealth, the active desire of children and adults to learn English – one of the official languages of each of the Commonwealth nations – was the basis of our decision to source stories and poems originally written in, or already translated into, English or English creole. I have included retellings of traditional tales by non-native authors alongside those of indigenous authors. Since customs of generational storytelling are gradually dying out, these retellings help disseminate tales that might otherwise become lost through lack of exposure. I have been humbled by the passion with which authors, teachers, librarians and scholars from many different cultures wish to see their countries' stories reach new readers. By including such tales, I hope to have created a transformative space for cross-cultural dialogue and opened up the lines of communication between different storytelling traditions.

The collection's real journey has just begun. From here we envisage its passage out into the world gaining momentum just as a river gathers its waters to flow into the sea. We hope to see the anthology become an effective teaching aid in schools throughout the Commonwealth through which children can enjoy learning about the values of cross-cultural connection, ecological sustainability and the power and importance of storytelling as a means of disseminating ideas, customs and histories as well as stimulating creative thought and encouraging the imagination. For children in communities who have little access to imaginative writing, a collection of this kind is an invaluable resource.

I hope I have done justice to the Commonwealth Education Trust's aspirations to create an anthology that children across the world can find relevant and entertaining, and to the creative visions of the fifty-four authors and poets who lend their voices to this collection. If you would like to support the anthology's journey to reach children throughout the Commonwealth, please visit the Trust's website: www.CET1886.org. There you can read more about my journey to create the anthology and learn about our plans for its future.

ABOUT THE ANTHOLOGIST

Alice Curry gained a First Class degree in English Language and Literature from Oxford University, England, where she was awarded the Nielson Scholarship, and a Master's degree in Children's Literature from Macquarie University, Australia, where she was awarded the Vice-Chancellor's Commendation and the Macquarie University Higher Degree Research Excellence Prize. In 2008 she became an Associate Lecturer in Children's Literature at Macquarie University and won an Australian Government-funded Research Scholarship to complete a PhD on environmentally aware fiction for children and young adults. She has since been awarded a Research Fellowship at the International Youth Library in Munich, Germany, home to the White Ravens literary awards, and has spent a semester as a visiting scholar at the University of Turku, Finland. She has presented papers at several international conferences, published articles in a number of academic journals and written a series of stories for a Hong Kong-based bilingual children's magazine. She is a seasoned traveller and looks forward to finding stories to retell wherever she goes.

Acknowledgements and Permissions

I would like to extend my personal thanks to Velma Pollard, former Head of the Education and English Department at the University of the West Indies, Dr. Cherrell Shelley-Robinson, Senior Lecturer and Acting Head of the Department of Library and Information Studies at UWI, Aisha Spenser, member of the academic and teaching staff in the Education and English Department at UWI, Professor John Stephens, Emeritus Professor in English at Macquarie University in Sydney, Ann Lazim, Specialist Librarian at the Centre for Literacy in Primary Education in London, Morag Styles, Professor of Children's Poetry at the University of Cambridge, Jean Williams, Executive Director of the South African book donation agency Biblionef, Tanya Barden, Rare Books and Special Collections Head Librarian at the University of Cape Town and Cosmas Mabeya, Administrator at the South African book donation agency The Bookery, as well as the wonderful Commonwealth Education Trust team, for their much appreciated help and advice in the making of this collection.

Alice Curry

The following lists the sources and permissions for the stories and poems found in this anthology.

Drawing Water from the Well

Barolong Seboni, 'Woman's World' (From 'An Anthology of Botswana Poetry in English'), Morula Publishers, Botswana 2002. Pleasant De Spain, 'Cooking with Salt Water' (From 'Eleven Nature Tales: A Multicultural Journey), August House Inc., Atlanta 1996. By permission of August House Inc. Emma Kruse Va'ai, 'Prescription' (From 'Whetu Moana: Contemporary Polynesian Poems in English), Auckland University Press, 2003. By permission of Emma Kruse Va'ai. Saviour Pirotta, 'Do you Believe in MAGIC?', Orion Publishing Group Ltd, London 1990. By permission of Orion Publishing Group Ltd. W.R.E. Clarke, 'Woman's World' (From 'Some Folk Tales of Sierra Leone'), Macmillan & Co. Ltd,

London 1963. KARLO MILA, *'Wednesday Afternoon'*, (From 'Whetu Moana: Contemporary Polynesian Poems in English), Auckland University Press, Auckland 2003. By permission of Karlo Mila-Schaaf. ANN WALTON, *'The Magic Fish'* (From 'Legends of the African Lakes: Tales from Malawi and the Great Lakes of Africa), Central Africana, Malawi 1997. By permission of Central Africana Ltd. BO FLOOD, BERET E. STRONG, WILLIAM FLOOD, *'Why People Have to Die'*, (From Pacific Island Legends: Tales from Micronesia, Melanesia, Polynesia and Australia), Bess Press Inc., Honolulu 1999. By permission of Bess Press Inc.

Down by the Waterhole
TOM NEVIN, *'The Enchanted River Tree'* & *'Nkalimeva'*, (From Zamani: African Tales from Long Ago), Jacaranda Designs, Kenya 1995. By permission of Jacaranda Designs. ASHLEY B. SAUNDERS, *'The March of the Hermit Crabs in the Rain'* (From 'Voyage into the sunset (Contemporary Poets of Dorrance Series)), Dorrance Publishing Co. Inc., Pennsylvania 1976. MAKERITA VAAI, *'Black Noddy'* (From 'Te Rau Maire: Poems and Stories of the Pacific), Tauranga Vananga (Ministry of Cultural Development), Cook Islands 1992. FRANCESCA MARTIN, *'Clever Tortoise: A Traditional African Tale'*, Walker Books, London 2001. By permission of Walker Books.

Waves Upon the Shore
ROMA POTIKI, *'When it's Summer'*, (From 'Whetu Moana: Contemporary Polynesian Poems in English), Auckland University Press, Auckland 2003. By permission of Roma Potiki. MEDERIC ADRIENNE, *'Kader'*, (From 'Indian Ocean Folk Tales: Madagascar, Comoros, Mauritius, Reunion, Seychelles'), National Folklore Support Centre, India, 2002. By permission of Prof. Lee Haring. RAYMOND BARROW, *'Dawn is a Fisherman'* (From 'Of Words: An Anthology of Belizean Poetry'), Cubola Productions, Benque Viejo 2006. MANEL RATNATUNGA, *'The Two Crabs'*, (From 'Folk Tales of Sri Lanka'), Sterling Publishers Pvt. Ltd, New Delhi 1980. By permission of Sterling Publishers Pvt. Ltd. KAY POLYDORE, *'The Sea is a Mystery to Me'* (From 'Pause to Ponder: Poems and Calypsoes'). By permission of Kay Polydore. JAMES BERRY, *'Seashell'* (From 'A Nest Full of Stars: Poems'), Pan Macmillan, England 2002. By permission of Macmillan Children's Books. CARL DE SOUZA, *'Citronella: A story from Mauritius'*, New African Education, Claremont 2001. By permission of New African Education. Translated from the French by Data and Decisions consulting.

The Salty Sea Breeze
TIMOTHY CALLENDER, *'The Legend of the Golden Apple Tree'*, (From 'Tales of the

Caribbean: Historical & Hysterical'), Realization Studios, St Kitts 2007. By permission of Mrs Lorna Callender. **SHAKE KEANE, 'Once the Wind'** (From 'Black Poetry'), Blackie Children's Books, London 1988. **MARGARET READ MacDONALD, 'Si Perawai, the Greedy Fisherman',** (The Singing Top: Tales from Malaysia, Singapore and Brunei'), Libraries Unlimited, Westport CT 2008. By permission of ABC-CLIO. **FARAH DIDI, 'Sailing under Moonlit Skies'** (From 'Emerging from Twilight - A Shadow Poetry Collection Vol. 2'), Infinity Publishing, Pennsylvania, USA. **JAN KNAPPERT, 'The Three Brothers',** (From 'The Book of African Tales'), The Edwin Mellen Press Ltd, Lewiston, NY 1999. By permission of The Edwin Mellen Press Ltd. **LENRIE PETERS,** excerpt from **'We Have Come Home',** (From 'The Penguin Book of Modern African Poetry [Third Edition]), Penguin Classics, Harmondsworth, England 1984. By permission of Pearson Education. **SHEILA WEE, 'Rajah Suran's Expedition to China'** By permission of Sheila Wee.

Sun, Moon and the Starry Sky
MERVYN SKIPPER, 'The Messenger of the Moon' (From 'The Meeting-Pool'), Puffin Books, London 1975. **ALTHEA TROTMAN, 'How the Starfish got to the Sea',** Sister Vision Press, Toronto 1992. **ZEHRA NIGAH, 'Right here was the Ocean'. NURUNNESSA CHOUDHURY, 'The Sun Witness',** (From 'Life Doesn't Frighten me at all'), Heinemann, 1998. By permission of Egmont UK Ltd. Translated from Bengali by Nurunnessa Choudhury and Paul Joseph Thompson. **M. P. ROBERTSON, 'The Moon in Swampland',** Frances Lincoln Children's Books, England 2004. By permission of Frances Lincoln Children's Books. **THOMAS H. SLONE, 'The Star's Tears',** (From 'One Thousand One Papua New Guinea Nights: Folktales from Wantok Newspaper – Vol 1: Tales from 1972-1985), Masalai Press, Oakland CA 2001. By permission of Thomas H. Slone. **CHRISTINE GUSTAVE, 'Being Free',** (From 'Against the Tides'). By permission of Christine Gustave.

Why a Rainbow Follows Rain
TAIA TEUAI, 'The Rain Maker' (From an untitled story by Taia Tevani - 'Tuvalu: A History'), Published jointly: Institute of Pacific Studies & Extension Services; University of the South Pacific & the Ministry of Social Services, Government of Tuvalu, Tuvalu 1983. **MPHO MAMASHELA, 'The Mist',** (From 'My African World: Poems for Younger Readers'), David Phillips Publishers, Cape Town 1996. By permission of Mpho Mamashela. **LINDA RODE, 'Rain and Fire'** (From 'In the Never-Ever Wood'), Tafelberg Publishers, Cape Town 2009. By permission of NB Publishers. **VERNA AARDEMA,** An excerpt from **'Bringing the Rain to Kapiti Plain',** Dial Press, NY 1981. By permission of Curtis Brown Ltd. **ASHOK B. RAHA**

(trans. Lila Ray), **'The Storm'** (From 'You'll Love This Stuff!: Poems from Many Cultures'), Cambridge University Press, Cambridge 1986. TRADITIONAL, **'Invocation to the Rainbow'** (From 'Anthologie de la Poesie Nego-Africaine pour la Jeunesse'), NEA/Edicef, Paris 1986. KATHLEEN ARNOTT, **'The Thunder Spirit's Bride'**, (From 'African Fairy Tales'), Fredrick Muller Ltd, London 1967. DAN DAVIS, **'Mookari'**, Queensland. By permission of Dan Davis.

Ghosts, Giants and Mermaids of the Deep

JOHN AGARD, **'Wind and River Romance'** (From 'Caribbean Poetry Now – 2nd Edition') Edward Arnold Publishers 1992. By permission of The Caroline Sheldon Literary Agency. M. NORBESE PHILIP, **'When I was a Child'** (From 'Thorns') Williams-Wallace, Canada 1980. By permission of M. NorbeSe Philip. BO FLOOD, BERET E. STRONG, WILLIAM FLOOD, **'Tebwere, Tebarere and Tetintiri'** (From 'Pacific Island Legends: Tales from Micronesia, Melanesia, Polynesia and Australia'), Bess Press Inc., Honolulu 1999. By permission of Bess Press Inc. CLARITA RICHARDS, **'The Enchanted Rock'** (From 'Poems & Stories of St. Christopher, Nevis & Anguilla') University College of the West Indies. BO FLOOD, BERET E. STRONG, WILLIAM FLOOD, **'Warrior Women of Lumalao'** (From 'Pacific Island Legends: Tales from Micronesia, Melanesia, Polynesia and Australia'), Bess Press Inc., Honolulu 1999. By permission of Bess Press Inc. NORA NADJARIAN, **'Kyrenia'**, Editions Rodopi B.V., Amsterdam 2004. By permission of Editions Rodopi B.V./Nora Nadjarian. NADRIEN MCINTYRE, **'Rampunch and the Sea Devil'**, (From 'Tim Tim Tales: Children's Stories from Grenada, West Indies'), University of the West Indies 1974. By permission of Veronica Nadica McIntyre.

Water Gods and Ice Kings

VIC PARKER, **'The Water God's Challenge'** (From 'Traditional Tales from Africa: based on myths and legends retold by Philip Ardagh'), Belitha Press Ltd, London 2001. ABENA P. A. BUSIA, **'Mawu of the Waters'** (From 'Talking Drums: A Selection of Poems from Africa South of the Sahara'), A & C Black, London 2001. By permission of Abena P. A. Busia. ROSETTA BASTERVILLE, **'The River Fairy'**, (From 'The Flame-Tree and Other Folk-Lore Stories from Uganda') The Sheldon Press, London, pre-1925. A. B. DEMILLE, **'The Ice King'**, (From 'The Wind Has Wings: Poems from Canada') Oxford University Press, 1968. MARGARET OLIVIA WOLFSON, **'Marriage of the Rain Goddess'**, Barefoot Books, Bath 1996. By permission of Barefoot Books.